CHRISTMAS AT THE MARSHMALLOW CAFE

CHRISTMAS AT THE MARSHMALLOW CAFE

CP WARD

"Christmas at the Marshmallow Cafe"
Copyright © CP Ward 2020

The right of Chris Ward to be identified as the Author of this Work has been asserted by him in accordance with the Copyright, Designs and Patents Act 1988.

All rights reserved. No part of this publication may be reproduced, stored in a retrieval system, or transmitted, in any form or by any means without the prior written permission of the Author.

This story is a work of fiction and is a product of the Author's imagination. All resemblances to actual locations or to persons living or dead are entirely coincidental.

BOOKS BY CP WARD

I'm Glad I Found You This Christmas
We'll have a Wonderful Cornish Christmas
Coming Home to Me This Christmas
Christmas at the Marshmallow Cafe

For John,
never one to turn down a marshmallow

PART I

SPECIAL LEFTOVERS

1
BOREDOM AMONG THE AISLES

A HUMAN BEING IN OUTER APPEARANCE ONLY, THE manager of the Weston super Mare branch of Morrico was rumoured to be everything from a devil in human clothing to a closet politician.

Bonnie Green looked up as the Old Ragtag bore down on her out of the colorful, brightly lit tea and coffee aisle, his bad leg scraping at the floor as he dragged it after him, his unruly hair leaping like poorly synchronized swimmers with each laborious step. His face, rather in keeping with his appearance, suggested some deep insult had been inflicted on his very being, and that someone needed to be punished.

Cyril Reeves looked down at the clipboard he always carried, even though no one in living memory could ever remember him writing anything down, and then back up at Bonnie, eyes narrowing behind the 1950s horn-rimmed spectacles he wore. Crouched beneath the checkout on a chair set too low—supermarket policy; Cyril claimed it made the customers feel more important—Bonnie tried to force a smile.

'Yes, Cyril?'

The Old Ragtag leaned on the counter then idly picked at a blemish on the stainless steel as though ordering the composites of metal and their imperfections was Bonnie's personal responsibility.

'I hear you were in the backroom when the music was changed. It's November the fourth. Why did you put on the Christmas songs CD? You know store policy. Christmas songs cannot be played until November 6th. November 5th inclusive is too close to Halloween.'

Bonnie groaned inwardly, but outwardly maintained a plastic smile. 'I do apologise, Cyril. I mistook the date.'

'See that it doesn't happen again.'

'Of course.' She gave him her best smile, the one she usually reserved for handsome young shoppers.

'Good. And by the way, I prefer Mr. Reeves while we're at work. Let's keep things formal, shall we? I wouldn't want to hit you with a disciplinary.' Then, in a moment which made Bonnie wish she hadn't eaten tuna sandwiches for lunch, Cyril winked. 'Cyril is fine at the staff Christmas party.'

As soon as his back was turned, Bonnie looked at Jean on the adjacent till and rolled her eyes. Jean covered her mouth to suppress a laugh as the Old Ragtag stumped off into the aisles, no doubt to terrorise some of the younger staff who were actually afraid of him, as though he were store manager by day, serial killer by night.

'Big ugly fish in a small, dirty pond,' Jean said.

'That we also happen to be stuck in,' Bonnie said. 'God forbid we allow any joy into our work lives.'

'You know,' Jean said, 'I picked up a job paper on the way out yesterday. Thought I might have a look.'

'Anything catch your fancy?'

Jean laughed. 'At my age? I'd be jumping out of one

fishbowl into another. Sometimes wish I'd made better decisions earlier in life.'

Bonnie nodded, understanding only too well. 'Me too.'

'Oh well, at least you're off in a few. I'm stuck with him until nine. You know he does double shifts almost every day?'

Bonnie nodded. She craned her head to see into the nearest aisle, where the Old Ragtag was berating some poor school kid for not properly lining up the biscuit packets. 'I'm pretty sure he'd doing a fiddle there. He just likes to terrorise us.'

Jean smiled, then turned away as a customer approached. Bonnie settled back into the position she had taken for granted for the last ten years, smiling as a lady with two sulky teenagers in tow approached.

'Gavin, can you please give me a hand with this?' she snapped at the boy, who was leaning over a handheld video game. Then, turning to the girl, she huffed, 'Eliza? Can you help me unload the trolley?'

With a sigh as loud as a departing steam train, the girl stomped over and began dumping food onto the conveyor with far more aggression than necessary. As Bonnie began to run up the items on the scanner, the woman gave her a smile.

'I suppose they're not teenagers for long,' she said. 'Once they hit their twenties I expect they'll turn back into normal human beings.'

Bonnie gave her a sympathetic smile and muttered a generic reply. *Sure, they will,* she thought. *And they'll go off and get on with their own lives and leave you behind.*

As she finished ringing up the woman's shopping, she couldn't help but notice the clock. Five to five. She was almost done. It was so nice to be on the day shift, to get to eat dinner at a reasonable time. She had nothing planned;

perhaps she'd stop by the chip shop on the way home, or even live it up a little and get a Chinese. The Peeking Duck takeaway on the high street did a great chow mein.

Both the chip shop and the Chinese were shut. There was another Chinese a fifteen minute drive away, but with her little Metro and its misfiring heating system stuck in traffic, Bonnie gave up. With roadworks contributing to the rush hour mess, she didn't get home until six-thirty. As she stumbled in through the door of her little terrace on Westing Road, she wasn't sure she could be bothered to eat at all.

She kicked away some circulars from the mat, took off her coat, and went into the living room. It was chilly even this early in November, so she turned on the heating and then slumped into an armchair without even taking off her shoes. She had already ditched her uniform at the supermarket—at one point Cyril had tried to distribute t-shirts with the company logo to be worn outside of work as a form of passive advertising, but the plan had fallen flat on its face—but she still liked to get out of the clothes she had worn underneath. They always smelled of the disinfectant everything was sprayed with, and mingled with her sweat, they were like wearing a bad memory.

Without moving, she tried to remember what food she had in the house. Some pasta. A jar of pickles Debbie had brought round and left. Perhaps there was a frozen pizza, but it was months old. Working in a supermarket gave Bonnie a particular dislike for the places, and without anyone to cook for, she rarely felt the need to stock up. Perhaps she could wander down the street to the greasy spoon and gorge on a plate of deep-fried heart attack. She was almost tempted until she remembered the last time she had gone down there. Sat in the window, a lonely fifty-something woman eating fried bread and sausages, a middle-aged man in a coat far more expensive than Bonnie could ever afford had come in off the street to ask her for a going rate.

She had been almost flattered before telling him where to go.

Since then she had always preferred to eat at home.

The TV remote was poking out of a crack in the corner of the sofa. It required at least three steps to reach it, then the additional effort of pressing the button to switch it on. And what for? It was Tuesday. Some glossy fly-on-the-wall show where everyone was young and beautiful? At least *Eastenders* was so miserable it made her happy about her own nothing of a life.

Perhaps it would be easier to just sit in the chair and wait until she decomposed. It had been months since Steve or Claire had so much as included her on an email circular, and even then it had probably been by mistake. They blamed her for their father's leaving, she knew. They always had, and over the years she had begun to believe them.

Fall asleep here in the armchair and never wake up. It would be months before anyone found her, years perhaps. She would be nothing more than a skeleton, or ideally, dust, so a simple vacuuming would erase her from existence. Her kids could throw her furniture out with the rubbish, and her landlord could rent out the property again.

Over. Gone. Done with.

BURRRRINNNGGGG—

Bonnie jumped as the door bell rang. Sometimes she forgot she even had one.

2

AN UNEXPECTED LETTER

Bonnie opened the door to find Debbie standing on the doorstep.

'Good, I'm glad you're home,' Debbie said. 'I need a heart-to-heart. I got dumped again.' She held up a plastic bag as though it would convince Bonnie. 'Did you eat yet? No? Good. I got a filthy vindaloo. Figured I was going to cry anyway. And I picked up a DVD from Save the Children. *Hachi*, with Richard Gere. Don't worry, he doesn't last long. It's all about the dog, which gets old and dies a sad, lonely death. Never cried so much. Might need to again. That work?'

Bonnie smiled. 'Sometimes I think you're my guardian angel.'

'Huh? You know there's no such thing. There might be a hell, but there's certainly no heaven. Hell, definitely. My whole life is in it.'

'Well, let's see what we can do.' Bonnie stepped back to allow her next-door neighbour's black-clad, greasy-haired niece into the house.

'Take the gear,' Debbie said, handing over the bag. 'Go

and heat up the naan a minute. They always go cold. Yours is the plain. Mine's the turmeric and ginger. I needed something to clear out the sniffles.'

Debbie gave a dramatic sniff as if to emphasise the point. Bonnie took the bag and headed for the kitchen, aware it would take Debbie a couple of minutes to unlace the knee-length boots she wore.

A few minutes later they sat across from each other at Bonnie's kitchen table. Debbie, having removed her trenchcoat like a beetle shedding its shell, wore a leather tunic over an Iron Maiden t-shirt, along with black jeans. She shoveled vindaloo into her mouth with a tablespoon, her forehead beaded with sweat, occasionally swiping the braids of dyed black hair out of her way. Bonnie, picking slowly through a curry so hot the aroma alone burned her lips, watched her best friend with an unavoidable sense of amusement.

'So, when do you want to tell me what happened with Ben?'

'Colm. Ben was last month. I've blocked his Twitter and everything.'

'Okay, Colm. Is that short for something?'

'Mark.'

Bonnie lifted an eyebrow. 'Is there a specific reason how Mark became Colm?'

Debbie looked up, the tunic laced too tight across her chest creaking with the movement. 'His name's Mark Briscol. Briscol, M. Get it?'

'What's that, from his prison record?'

Debbie scowled. 'He only had an ASBO. And that was only because he got mad at his grandmother's cat. It took a dump on his car windscreen.'

'So he cleaned it with a chainsaw?'

'Are you taking the Mickey?'

Bonnie waited until Debbie turned to grab a handful of naan before she let herself smile. 'Would I?'

'Yeah, you would. You think I'm like some comedy show.'

Bonnie shook her head. 'I take every word you say with deadly seriousness. So, what happened?'

Debbie finished off her last spoonful of vindaloo and let out a belch, catching herself with a pardon just in time.

'That filled a hole,' she said. 'Right, I was talking about Colm?'

'Yeah.'

'He dumped me. Right in the middle of the dancefloor at Kevil's.'

'The rock club?'

'Yeah. Sweat pit, that place is. Hell. You going to finish that?'

Bonnie smiled and passed across the remains of her vindaloo, taking her plain naan before Debbie could lay claim to it too. 'Go for it.'

'Thanks. So, I'm on the dancefloor, and I'm getting into some Judas Priest, and you know, I'd put some ball bearings into my braids just to keep them straight. Colm reckoned I punched him but it was just the hair, you know?'

'You got a little excited.'

'Yeah. And so he said he wanted someone who was a little more of a lady. I mean, who does he think he is? That One Direction-liking pri—'

'I'm sure he didn't mean it like that,' Bonnie interrupted.

'I saw the CD in his car. He tried to pretend it was his little sister's, like he'd had to put it on for her when he dropped her off at ballet class.' Debbie loaded another heap of vindaloo into her mouth, then coughed, managing to hold her mouth closed but appearing for a few seconds to go into some kind of sudden seizure. Bonnie leaned across and patted her on the back until she had got herself under control.

'Men are all scum,' Debbie said at last, her face red. Sometimes I wish I batted for the other side. 'Let's open the wine.'

'That sounds like a great idea,' Bonnie said. 'Did you bring any?'

Debbie shook her head. 'Nah. Just a couple of cans of Guinness. I was thinking about you. Fifty-odd and divorced, you must have wine. How else are you supposed to get through the evenings?'

'That's a good question. I'm afraid I must have finished it off drowning my sorrows last night.'

Debbie shrugged. 'Not to worry. I'll spot you a can. If we need to carry on I'll do a booze run down to the corner shop later. I know the kid who works nights. I got him some Cinderella tickets last summer.'

'The musical?'

Debbie shook her head. 'The eighties hair-metal band. Reunion tour. They suck. Got them free with a magazine and would have thrown them away but we were talking and he said he'd never been to a concert. I figured it was best to start low.'

'He didn't like it?'

Debbie scowled. 'Have you seen his hair? Looks like he's got a dead cat on his head. Thinks they're the best band in the world. Fourteen and I've already ruined him.' She shrugged. 'Oh well, kid loves me now. Always knocks a couple of quid off.'

They cleared away the plates and moved to the living room. Debbie loaded the DVD into the player and sat back on the sofa, pulling the coffee table over so she could put up her feet—black socks with red devil logos on the ankles. The casualness of her manner never ceased to make Bonnie laugh; she sometimes wished everyone could go through life with the same casual ignorance of social rules. Debbie was a walking stereotypical trainwreck, but since the night Bonnie had found Debbie banging drunkenly on her door—the girl having mistaken in which house she lived upon returning after a rock club bender—they had been best friends. Debbie and her endless dramas was a nostalgic reminder for Bonnie of the youth that somewhere along the line she had left far behind.

The DVD had loaded up its start screen, a little dog icon hovering over START MOVIE. Debbie swigged from her can of Guinness and sighed.

'Honestly, sometimes I'm envious of you,' she said, swinging her head to look at Bonnie, who hadn't yet opened her can. 'I mean, you're what? Fifty-five, single, a homeowner, your kids leave you alone—'

Bonnie lifted a hand. 'Just to make a couple of clarifications there … I'm fifty-two. Yes, I'm single, but I'm also divorced, which is like having a medal around your neck with "worthless" written on it. My husband ran off with a hat saleswoman he met when he was buying me a hat for Christmas because he didn't like my hair and wanted something to cover it on the rare occasions we ever went out. I'm a homeowner only because he took all our savings in the divorce in exchange for letting me keep the house … and the mortgage I can barely pay on my pathetic Morrico salary. And both my kids took his side. Said I should have dressed better. I'm lucky if I get a card for my birthday now.'

Debbie stared at her for a long time. Finally an eyebrow lifted. 'I know all that,' she said. 'I was paraphrasing for the sake of clarity.'

'Thanks. Can't you paraphrase my age downwards in future?'

'Fifty-five can be anything in the fifties, but if I say you're forty-nine that's an outright lie.'

Bonnie shrugged. Lifting the can of Guinness, she swallowed as much as she could in a single gulp. It was only about a quarter of the can, but it took her so long that Debbie gave a respectful nod.

'We need more booze,' she said. 'I'll go.'

'I'll come with you.'

At the door, Debbie kicked the cluster of circulars into a pile and scooped them up. 'Shall I dump them into next door's dustbin on the way out? You know clutter just bugs me. I think it's my OCD.'

'Next door's is your mother's.'

'On the other side.'

'Sure.'

Debbie gave the letters a quick shuffle as though looking for any coupons. She frowned and lifted an official letter which had been hidden at the bottom.

'Oooh. Franklin & Sons. A letter from a lawyer. Perhaps you're being repossessed.'

'Let me take a look. It's probably just advertising.'

Debbie stood patiently as Bonnie ripped open the letter, unfolded it, and skim-read the contents. Reaching the bottom, she frowned, then read it over again.

'I don't believe it,' she said.

3
A TREASURED MEMORY

DEBBIE HAD GONE FOR THE BOOZE, PROMISING TO BRING back 'something girly' for Bonnie in addition to whatever black-coloured liquid she planned on getting for herself. Bonnie sat on the sofa, reading the letter over and over, still not believing that it was real, and if it was, what she was going to do about it.

She barely even remembered Uncle Mervin. He was her dad's older brother, but the most recent occasion she could remember meeting him had been when she was twelve. Not that they'd had much interaction; he had stopped in for a coffee with her mother on his way to somewhere and Bonnie had been called out of her room to say a brief hello.

Forty years ago.

In the years since she didn't think he'd ever crossed her mind.

By some randomness of fate and family trees, he had died and left her all his worldly possessions.

Well, sort of.

Had he left her a lump sum it might have been useful,

but according to the lawyer's deeds, the most prominent thing he had left her was the remainder of a hundred-year lease on a business.

A shop, to be exact.

The lawyer's letter was maddening light on detail, providing only basic information. The business was described as retail: confectionary. An address, somewhere in the Lake District. At least the location sounded nice. The details of the lease described the shop as being part of a larger retail park, the lease one that while technically lasting a lifetime, could not be sold, only given away upon its leaseholder's death.

The door went, Debbie returning. After removing her coat and shoes—she had borrowed a pair of Bonnie's trainers for the short trip to the corner shop because 'the coat'll cover them in the dark'—she marched into the living room and held up a plastic bag.

'I got you some red.'

'Wine?'

Debbie grinned. 'Aftershock. No, only joking, yeah, course it's wine. It was on special so I got you two bottles. And biscuits. Yours are plain, mine are the dark chocolate chip.' She started to sit down before noticing the letter. 'Oh, did you read it? Do tell.'

Bonnie paraphrased the contents. 'So, basically, a relative I can barely remember has left me a property I'm not allowed to sell.'

'Sweet. In the Lake District? Do they have pubs up there?'

'I would imagine so.'

'Awesome. So, what kind of shop is it?'

'Confectionary.'

'Which is what?'

Bonnie held up a chocolate bar. 'You're looking at it.'

'Cool. So, you're going to quit your job and go and run it?'

Bonnie frowned. She hadn't yet thought about what she was going to do. She figured that in the morning she would have to call the lawyer and talk over the finer details. Sure, she was in receipt of the property, but did that mean she had to pay rates or taxes on it? What had at first seemed like a surprise windfall was looking more like a monkey on her back. The Lake District was at the other end of the country. She couldn't just drop everything and drive up there, assuming, of course, her little Metro could even survive the journey. The Old Ragtag prohibited any personal days off between October and Christmas, and the way her shifts were spread out meant she'd have to be up and back in a thirty-six hour window.

Debbie was still staring at her. 'Well?'

'I don't know. I don't know enough about it to make that kind of decision. The pig I used to be married to left me with a mortgage on this place and nothing in the bank. If I quit my job I'll lose my house.'

'You said you had an address, didn't you? Let's have a look on the net and see if we can get a bit more info.'

'All right.'

Bonnie retrieved the old laptop she rarely used from a cupboard and loaded it up. Debbie sniggered as an ancient-looking Windows XP logo appeared.

'Like watching a calving glacier,' Debbie said. 'Are you sure you don't need to wind it up a bit more?'

After a painstaking age of waiting for the computer to load, during which time Debbie sank two cans of stout and Bonnie a glass and a half of wine, they finally got online. Debbie pulled up a map program and after another age of waiting for everything to load, they found an aerial view of the property.

'It's in some kind of theme park,' Debbie said. 'Look, that wiggly thing is either a giant snake or a rollercoaster, and I reckon the news would have mentioned a giant snake. Let's see if we can get a street view. Jesus, if I'd have known it would take six years to load, I would have gone and got my smartphone.'

'I don't have much use for technology,' Bonnie said, giving Debbie a wink. 'I'm a grandmother, don't you know?'

'Ah, you're doing all right,' Debbie said. 'Wow, look at that. Good god, is this some kind of a joke?'

The street view had appeared. A medieval-styled building stood in the foreground, a café premises large enough to have a living area attached. It's pointed roof, black and white design and faux wooden eaves made both Bonnie and Debbie coo with excitement.

'That's totally convertible into a rock club,' Debbie said.

'Can you zoom in on the sign over the door?'

'Hang on a sec.'

The view enlarged. Bonnie let out a chuckle as the sign over the entrance came into focus. The writing was all gothic, but the meaning was not.

Mervin's Marshmallow Café.

'What's that small line over the top?' Debbie said. 'Welcome to—'

Bonnie almost dropped her glass, catching it with her other hand and receiving a slosh of wine over her fingers. 'I don't believe it,' she said. 'All these years … and it did exist after all.'

'What?'

Bonnie wiped away a tear, thinking of long ago evenings when her dad would tell her stories before bed. Sat in a chair beside her, his hands would gesture wildly as he told her fantastical tales of a place he had claimed was real and would one day take her. It had never happened, her dad dying of cancer when she was twelve. That would have been the reason for Uncle Mervin's last visit, now that she thought about it; her dad's funeral. His death had left Bonnie heartbroken; while she treasured the memories she had of him, she had locked them away to keep them safe, in the same way she had let go of the name of the semi-mythical place.

Christmas Land.

4

ELOPEMENT PLANS

DEBBIE SPAT BEER ALL OVER THE CARPET, DRAWING A scowl from Bonnie. 'Christmas Land? Are you having a laugh? You've inherited a marshmallow café in a theme park called Christmas Land? Come on, this is hilarious.'

'My dad used to tell me stories about it,' Bonnie said. 'He said it was in the north, and it was the most magical place in the world. He said it was a place you could visit all year round, but the true magic only happened at Christmas. When snow blanketed the ground, herds of reindeer would run among the shops and rides, and on Christmas Eve, Father Christmas himself would arrive, to hand out presents to all the visitors. He said that one day, when I was old enough to truly appreciate its magic, we would all go together.'

'I'm guessing you never got there,' Debbie said. 'What happened?'

'My dad died. Mum struggled to makes ends meet, so I worked part time after school. We didn't really have any magic in our family after that. We got by, we loved each other, but life wasn't easy.'

Debbie shook her head. 'Life sucks,' she said. 'We're literally put here to suffer.'

'And then we go to heaven, right?'

Debbie shook her head. 'Hell. Just to rub it in that we spent all that time feeling miserable, when in actually fact, that torment was the good part.' She shrugged. 'At least they should have decent music down there.'

Bonnie smiled. 'Dad never mentioned Uncle Mervin actually lived at Christmas Land,' she said. 'No wonder he never visited. He probably couldn't bear to leave.'

Debbie leaned over the computer. 'Let's check out the online reviews of this place,' she said, grimacing as a reviews website took its time to load. 'Ah, here we are. "If I could give it zero I would." "Most rides were closed." "Dirty, litter everywhere." "Father Christmas was drunk and threw up over my kid." "Overpriced and understaffed." "They should bulldoze it. A landfill would be more exciting." "The so-called turkey was chicken and it gave me food-poisoning." "Christmasless Land."' She looked up at Bonnie. 'What do you think?'

Bonnie grimaced. 'It doesn't sound too promising, does it?'

'You reckon?' Debbie's eyes gleamed. 'It sounds absolutely awesome. Come on, you totally have to jack in your job and go check it out. I'll come with you if you like. I need to get my dole check just after nine but we can leave straight after.' She nudged Bonnie's arm. 'Come on. You know you want to.'

Bonnie closed her eyes. From as young as she could remember up until her father's death, she had dreamed of visiting Christmas Land. Forty years later, she now knew it existed, and she even had a reason to go. But … could she? There was no way the place could ever live up to the images that had once filled her head. She was headed for certain disappointment.

'I'll call the lawyer tomorrow,' she said. 'I'll see if there's some way I can donate the lease to charity or leave it in a trust. The whole thing is just silly. I can't just take off halfway across the country on a whim. It's not … me.'

Debbie put her beer can down on the coffee table with a crack loud enough to make Bonnie jump. Swiping braids out of her eyes, Debbie shook her head.

'Did I just hear you correctly?'

'Yes—'

'Come on, Bon. Stop thinking like an old fart.'

'What?'

'You've got to think like the youth.' Debbie poked herself in the tunic with one black-fingernailed thumb. 'Think like me.'

'I'm not sure that—'

'You don't have to quit your job just to go and take a look. Pull a sickie. Or two. Or take a whole week. You have influenza. We'll get my dole cheque, then we'll drive up and check this place out, see what we make of it.'

'I need a sick note to take a week off with flu.'

Debbie grinned. 'You can get one off the internet. Well, not this internet, but one that works. I'll print one off and bring it over in the morning. Until then, though, might be a good idea to look a bit sick, just in case your boss calls.' She held up her can. 'Down the hatch.'

Bonnie grimanced. 'I'm fifty-two years old, I don't do down the hatch.'

'Well, take a matronly sip then.'

Bonnie lifted her glass. 'I must be out of my mind letting you talk me into this,' she said, taking as big a sip as she could handle. 'When I got up this morning, I had no idea I'd be getting drunk with a girl young enough to be my daughter and planning to take off after a childhood dream.'

'I didn't talk you into it,' Debbie said. 'I just gave you room to convince yourself. It's basic psychology, you know, brains and stuff? Delay the no long enough and it turns into a yes.'

'Is that really ethical?'

Debbie shrugged. 'Who knows? Are you going to eat those biscuits or not?'

5

ON THE ROAD

THE WAY BONNIE FELT THE NEXT MORNING, SHE MIGHT as well have had influenza. She crawled out of bed, threw up in the bathroom and then staggered downstairs just in time to answer her doorbell.

Debbie stood there, a suitcase at her feet. 'Ready?'

'Huh? I just got up.'

With a sigh, Debbie marched inside and begun painstakingly unlacing her boots. 'Don't just stand there,' she said, catching Bonnie watching. 'Make coffee. I'll pack for you.'

'How do you know what I'll need?'

Debbie rolled her eyes. 'I have a mother, don't I? The same stuff I'd have to pack for her.'

Fifteen minutes later, Debbie came back down the stairs carrying a suitcase. Bonnie had managed to shower and change, and had returned to the kitchen table to nurse her hangover over a second cup of coffee.

'Right, you're all ready,' Debbie said.

Bonnie looked up, trying to focus. Stumbling up to bed sometime after one a.m., she had forgotten to take out her contact lenses. Now, peering through the glasses she rarely wore, she wished the world would stop swaying from side to side.

'What did you pack for me?'

'Underwear and a jacket. We can pick anything else we'll need up on the way. They'll have charity shops in the Lake District.'

'Charity shops?'

Debbie glared at her and lifted her arms. 'You think this comes from the corporate machine? Free trade, baby. Charity shops and the net. I wouldn't be seen dead shopping anywhere else.'

'I would. In fact, I could handle death right about now.'

'Well, we're going in your car so it'll be nearby, that's for sure. You sure we can't go on B-roads?'

'It'll take a week to get there.'

'Ah, but Stephen King says it's all about the journey.'

'That's only because he can't write endings.'

'*Dark Tower* rocked. He must have had balls like a space hopper to dare pull that after seven books. Respect.'

'*Dreamcatcher* sucked.'

'Ah, but *Dreamcatcher* isn't classic era. It doesn't count.'

Bonnie lifted a tired hand. 'Okay. We can discuss Stephen King on the way.' Despite her hangover, she was quite excited about a long drive with Debbie. While their music tastes were polar opposites, they were perfectly aligned when it came to books. So much so, that they often swapped books they had recently read, or warned each other off books which had fallen short of expectations.

'Let's move. I need to be outside the job centre at nine. Did you call off work yet?'

'Not yet. I don't start until eleven.'

'Good. Let's get on the road before you do it. That way you can't chicken out.'

~

An hour later they were heading north through gradually thinning traffic. Debbie, wearing a smug grin after collecting her dole cheque far more quickly than usual, and managing to escape with an offhand 'I've been applying for jobs,' rather than be submitted to the usual interrogation, pointed at a service area sign.

'There,' she said. 'Mickey D's. I need breakie.'

'I thought you didn't do corporations?'

Debbie shrugged. 'I make exceptions for food. The taste alone is punishment enough.'

Bonnie pulled off the motorway and into the service area. While she couldn't quite face the same stack of hamburgers Debbie procured from MacDonald's, she felt a little better after a couple of sandwiches from a bakery. Sitting in a communal restaurant seating area, she finished her sandwich and sighed.

'I'm getting too old for this. This is what young people do.'

Debbie shrugged. 'You can consider it kidnap if it makes you feel better.'

'I suppose being kidnapped by a vampire is definitely something for the bucket list.'

Debbie stuffed one last hamburger into her mouth, manipulating it to get the whole thing inside at once. Bonnie stared at the figure squeezed into the leather tunic. There were fashion models more overweight than Debbie. With a smile she gave a bemused shake of the head.

Behind them, a chair scraped as a group of three lads got up. All designer jumpers and *Men's Health* haircuts, they looked on their way to an audition for Love Island. One of them glanced over his shoulder and noticed Bonnie and Debbie sitting nearby.

'Hey, Sharon Osborne!' he called, as the others laughed. 'Can you sign my bum cheek?'

Debbie, still chewing around a hamburger, glared at him. 'I'll sign it with a rusty harpoon,' she shouted.

'Ooh,' the first lad said, as the others laughed again. 'Hey, Grandma, better tie your dog up to your wheelchair.'

Debbie grabbed a plate and lifted it like a frizbee. 'I keep human heads as prizes,' she snapped, shaping to throw. Clearly alarmed, the lads backed away through the tables, their laughter turned nervous. Debbie, a snarl on her face, held the pose until they'd headed back out into the car park.

'I bet your mum feels safe with you around,' Bonnie said. 'Better than a guard dog.'

Debbie sat back down. 'I could have taken them,' she said. 'I was school discus champion.'

Bonnie lifted an eyebrow. 'For once, you surprise me. You, doing sports?'

'I mended the error of my ways after I bought my first Sabbath album,' Debbie said.

'So you considered being called Sharon Osborne a compliment?'

Debbie scowled. 'She's about nine hundred years old.'

'From the look of you, you could be too.'

Debbie rolled her eyes. 'Come on, *Grandma*. Let's get back on the road.'

A couple of hours later, after they had just got through roadworks outside Birmingham, Bonnie let out a sudden cry, thumping the wheel as she did so and beeping the horn by accident. She lifted a hand as the driver of the car in front gave her a middle finger.

'Look at that butt hole,' Debbie said. 'We should run him off the road. What's the matter?'

'I forgot to call in sick.'

Debbie grinned. 'We've got this. Next service area.'

'They pulled in at a small services and Bonnie took out her phone. Her hands were shaking; she was half an hour late already. She typed in the supermarket's number while beside her Debbie sniggered at her ancient phone. Scowling, Bonnie lifted it to her ear.

'I supposed it doesn't have a speaker, so I can't listen in,' Debbie said.

'Just be quiet a minute.'

'Hello? Morrico, Western-Super-Mare branch, store manager Cyril Reeves speaking. How may I be of assistance?'

Bonnie faked a cough. 'Um, hi Cyril ... uh, Mr. Reeves. It's Bonnie. I'm afraid I can't make it in today. I'm sick. I think I have flu.'

'What? You've never taken a day sick in seven years. In 2014 you even worked for six days with a plaster cast on your ankle. What's going on?'

Bonnie scowled. Trust the old fart to know. He hadn't even been working there that long, yet he somehow knew her historical record. She'd got drunk on cheap wine in the aftermath of her husband leaving and tripped on the front step. The doctor had signed her off for a week but she couldn't bear the thought of being in her empty house all alone, so she had staggered into work.

'I don't want to pass it on. The doctor's given me a note.'

'Well, can you drop it in?'

'Um, I'll get someone to stop by later. It's highly contagious.'

'It's a piece of bloody paper.'

'The flu, I mean.'

'All right, well, take care of yourself. We'll see you in a few days.'

'Thanks.'

She hung up, then leaned back in the seat, breathing out a sigh of relief.

'Boom,' Debbie said. 'I told you it was easy. The day you bend to the corporate machine is the day your soul dies.'

'He said we'll see you in a few days.'

'Nice. You're good to next Monday at least, and then we'll assess the situation. We might have to upgrade you to swine flu, or failing that, the bubonic plague.'

'Can you get doctors' notes for that?'

Debbie grinned. 'You can get everything on the internet.'

They set off again, leaving the smoke and urban sprawl of Birmingham behind. Countryside spread out around them as they headed further north. Debbie began to doze against the window, the ball-bearings in her hair rattling against the glass. Bonnie, keeping the Metro at a steady sixty—the fastest she could go without fearing it would fall apart—gazed out at the rolling hills on either side of the motorway, trying to remember if she'd ever been this far north before. As Debbie began to snore, the tales her father had told her about Christmas Land slowly began to return.

'There's a lake in the centre in the design of a heart. In winter it freezes over, and the water becomes as icy-blue as the sky. If you get up just before dawn and look out of the window, you'll see elves in green and gold racing across it, enjoying themselves before heading to the toy workshops to begin their day's work.'

Bonnie smiled. When she looked back on it now, the stories were cringe-worthy, storybook fantasy. At the time, though, she had hung on her father's every word.

'When you first awake and draw back the curtains of your chalet, you'll immediately be blinded by the snow glittering off the trees as the sun rises. Despite the cold—far colder than you could ever expect in England, because this is a special place, remember—you must certainly open your window, and drop a few seeds out onto the window ledge for the local robins. Each chalet has a resident bird which will surely come to see you. While not quite tame enough to touch, it will still give you the honour of its company before it sets off on its errands for the day. And then, listen quietly, for in the still of the morning before the park really wakes up, you can hear the reindeer calling each other among the trees.'

Bonnie sighed and wiped a tear from her eye. At the end of each story, he had left her with the same promise.

'And when you're old enough to appreciate it, we'll all go to Christmas Land together, where you can experience the magic of Christmas at any time of the year.'

He had died before fulfilling his promise. Bonnie didn't blame him, of course, but he had taken the magic of her childhood with him to the grave. The real world had rushed in, filling her life with the chores of washing plates and picking up dirty glasses, stuffing soiled sheets into industrial washers and scrubbing the crust off toilets. She had saved enough to pay her way into college and had dreamed of becoming a nurse. Donald had wanted her as a stay-at-home mum, however, and she had been happy, raising her children. She hadn't even noticed that none of his promises—of a better life, a nicer street, a bigger house and a newer car—ever materialised. At least not for her. He had saved plenty to keep his new hat lady happy, leaving Bonnie as a forty-something with no qualifications forced to sit behind a checkout at

Morrico to keep her head above the waters of her mortgage.

And the worst thing was that her children blamed her for everything.

She was still reminiscing on the past when a large white billboard came up on the left-hand side.

CHRISTMAS LAND
WHERE DREAMS COME TRUE
14 MILES – TURN LEFT NEXT JUNCTION

Bonnie shoved Debbie to wake her, slowing the car at the same time.

'Look,' she said, pointing as they passed the billboard, its chipped paint and one rusted metal leg horrifyingly apparent. Someone had thrown a bag of trash at it at some point, and now a plastic supermarket bag hung from a splinter of wood next to the word TRUE. It felt like a sign, all right.

As Debbie groaned, her head lolling, Bonnie thought it better to let her go back to sleep.

6

STUCK IN THE MUCK

AFTER TAKING THE JUNCTION FOR CHRISTMAS LAND, Bonnie began to see more signs. The landscape had changed, becoming beautiful, all rolling hills and moorland as they entered the Lake District. In the distance she caught glimpses of glittering water whenever they crested a rise. After a while she nudged Debbie awake. The younger girl looked up blearily, grinned, and said, 'Are we there yet?'

'Not yet, but nearly. Isn't it pretty?'

Debbie looked around. 'Where did all the hedges go?'

Dry stone walls had replaced the grassy hedgerows, the roads narrowing in many places to a single lane punctuated by small passing places.

'It's so charming,' Bonnie said, unable to keep a grin off her face. 'All these hills and lakes—'

'Fells and meres, Bon,' Debbie said.

Bonnie frowned. 'What? You fell where?'

Debbie shook her head. 'The hills are called "fells", and they call the lakes "meres", "waters" or "tarns".'

'Well, aren't you the expert?'

Debbie grinned. '*Countryfile*. Got to do something with my unemployment. You know, when I was a kid growing up, I used to fantasize about John Craven dressing in black and fronting a goth band.'

'So no My Little Ponies, then?'

'Had one once. I cut off its hair and painted it red.'

'I bet you were popular in playschool.'

Debbie grinned. 'No one ever pushed me off the slide.'

They passed another Christmas Land sign, poking out of an overgrown verge. Someone had scrawled *Father Christmas is dead* in red paint diagonally across it. Debbie glanced at Bonnie and raised an eyebrow.

'So it looks like this mythical place really does exist.'

'Well, it did, at least.'

'Sounds like my kind of place,' Debbie said.

'I'd turn back, but the tank's low and I haven't seen a petrol station in miles,' Bonnie said. 'I'm counting on them to have one.'

'All or nothing,' Debbie said. 'Have you seen *Deliverance*?'

Bonnie groaned. 'Of course I have.'

'What about *Wrong Turn*?'

Bonnie shook her head. 'I'm not familiar with that one.'

'It's about these kids who break down and end up caught by a family of rednecks—'

Bonnie put up a hand. 'I can imagine. Can't we talk about mince pies or something?'

'There's a man flagging us down up ahead,' Debbie said.

'Is he wearing a Christmas hat?'

'No, but he has some kind of stick.'

Debbie was right. An old man in Wellington boots, a tweed jacket and a flat cap was waving a stick at the car.

'Lock the doors,' Debbie said.

'Don't worry,' Bonnie said. 'I think it's just a local farmer.' She pulled up alongside the man and wound down the window. 'Is everything all right?'

'Cows coming through,' the man said. 'Might wanna pull a little thing like this over to that passing place there.'

All Bonnie saw was a patch of grass verge slightly wider than the rest. Grimacing, she backed her car up while Debbie stared with horror as the road ahead filled with trotting, jostling cattle.

'They'll crush us,' she gasped, opening the door to get out, but Bonnie, laughing put a hand on her arm.

'Just relax,' she said. 'You're safer inside.' She reached across and pulled Debbie's door shut, cutting off the head of a large thistle which landed on Debbie's lap. The girl stared at it, eyes wide.

'It's a sign,' she said.

'It's the country,' Bonnie said, as the nearest cows bumped past, a couple pressing against the window. One, pushed into their way by the others, actually put its front hooves up on the bonnet, before slipping off and turning on its way. Another, backing up against them, lifted its tail and let rip with a cascade of brown sauce all over the rear driver's side window.

'Oh, that's rank,' Debbie said.

'Isn't that your thing?' Bonnie asked. 'You know, biting the heads off chickens and all that?'

'We don't take a dump on someone's car,' Debbie said, nose wrinkling.

The parade lasted for several minutes, but finally it came to an end. A couple of darting sheepdogs brought up the rear, followed by a young boy who had to be the old man's grandson. He gave them a cheerful wave as he walked past.

'I suppose they don't have schools round here,' Debbie said.

'Only the school of life,' Bonnie answered. 'Might do you some good.'

Debbie ignored her. 'You reckon we might get another service area before we get there? I need to take a leak.'

Bonnie cringed. 'I doubt it.'

She let off the handbrake and put the car into gear, but when she engaged the accelerator, all she heard was the spinning of the rear wheels.

'Please don't tell me we're stuck,' Debbie said.

'We're stuck.'

Bonnie climbed out then helped Debbie to climb over the gearbox and out of the driver's side. The back wheels of the car were deep in boggy mud. Bonnie looked at Debbie and grinned.

'Part of the adventure,' she said.

Debbie shook her head. 'One of us—by default me, since it's your car—could get in there and push, and get absolutely covered in crap … or we could just call an Uber.'

'A what?'

'An Uber. It's like a private taxi service. People use their own cars to make money on the side.' She pulled her smartphone out of her pocket and held it up. 'Awesome. No signal. Right. You go for help, and I'll stay with the car.'

Bonnie shook her head. 'You talked me into this. We'll both go.'

'But what if we see some more cows?'

Bonnie shrugged. 'I don't know, we'll climb a tree or something.'

'There aren't any. It's all moor.'

'Then we'll climb up one of these stone walls and have a look. Come on, where's your sense of adventure?'

'This isn't quite what I imagined.'

'Are you scared?'

'No!' Debbie shrugged. 'Okay, I'll just get my CDs.' She leaned back into the car, retrieved a CD carry case and made it disappear somewhere inside her coat. 'Will we need weapons?'

'Why, what have you got hidden in there?'

Debbie pulled out a small black rectangle. 'I've got a taser.'

Bonnie laughed. 'I'm sure that'll be fine.'

They set off along the road. The last sign Bonnie remembered seeing had said three miles. As the road meandered between towering hedgerows broken by occasional gates giving a glimpse of farmland, she wondered if they had a different scale of measurement out here in the countryside. The walk wasn't unpleasant, though. Bonnie couldn't remember the last time she'd breathed air so fresh, and her ears had been unencumbered by the constant clatter of voices or traffic. Beside her, even Debbie had gone quiet, the black-clad girl huffing a little, but with the hint of a smile on her face.

Finally, they crested a rise, and found themselves looking downhill at a little village nestled in a forested valley. A church stood in the centre, tall trees filling its grounds like the leaves around a bouquet. A few houses were visible, but the village was so quaint and compact it looked like it would sit in the palm of one's hand.

'Is that it?' Debbie said. 'It's prettier than I'd expected, but I don't see any fairground rides.'

And after your hot chocolate and warm toast drenched in delicious local butter, why not try the forest coaster for your first thrill of the day? Winding through the trees among herds of wandering reindeer and culminating in a jaw-dropping loop, it's a Christmas thrill like no other.

Bonnie shook her head. 'I don't think this is it,' she said.

Around the next bend in the road they passed a sign.

WELCOME TO QUIMBECK
Enjoy your visit
Take nothing but photographs
Leave nothing but memories

'Sounds delightful,' Debbie said, rolling her eyes. Then, turning to Bonnie, she grinned. 'But I see something that'll perk us up. Look, there between those trees, just a couple of doors down from the church.'

Bonnie squinted. 'What? Your eyes are better than mine.'

'Salvation,' Debbie said. 'A pub.'

'Where?'

'There. The King's Thistle. That'll do.'

They walked down into the village, all narrow cobblestone streets packed with local craft shops, with a pretty river flowing through its centre. Bonnie saw several groups of ducks, and even a pair of swans.

'We could just stay here a few days,' she said. 'It seems pleasant enough. I'm sure they've got a B&B somewhere.'

Quimbeck was clearly a tourist village on the Lake District's hiking circuit, because they passed several groups of middle-aged hikers all in recently purchased gear, striding up and down the roads alongside the river and clustering outside the trinket shops and cafés. For Bonnie, who had spent her whole life being a dutiful and later rejected wife as well as an attentive and later rejected mother, and as a result had rarely ventured outside the town she grew up in, it was a delightful sight. She only wished she'd dressed a little better for it. In jeans and a Morrico own-brand jumper she felt at least half as wealthy as anyone they passed. When one elderly gentleman actually said 'How do you do?' as they passed and tipped a fisherman's hat, she turned to Debbie and shook her head.

'I think I want to go home,' she said.

'Why? We only just arrived. I'm only just getting movement back in my bum after sitting in your car for the last fifty years.'

'I feel so out of place.'

'Excuse me?' Debbie spread her arms. 'I am literally the walking dead. No one's looking at you because they're too scared to look away from me. Come on, let's get a pint and see if we can find someone who'll tow your car.'

They headed for the pub. A sign indicated a beer garden to the rear, but after one quick glance, Debbie shook her head. 'Toffs,' she said. 'A sea of them. We'll sit inside.'

The darker confines of a pub that proudly claimed to be over four hundred years old seemed to cater more to locals than to the steady stream of tourists. The beer garden turned out to be the overflow seating for a restaurant at the rear, which also had an attached bar area. Staying in the main bar, though, Debbie pointed to a narrow window seat between two fruit machines. From the scored and scarred table they could see the street, where couples and small groups ambled up and down narrow alleyways between old stone buildings, sometimes pausing to peer at a guidebook or map.

'A pint of Murphy's,' Debbie said to the landlord, a tall, balding man wearing a crisp blue shirt.

The man frowned. 'Don't have that, I'm afraid. Got a solid local version, Water Brown. That do?'

Debbie grinned. 'Sounds great.'

'Got it. And for your mother?'

Debbie sniggered. 'She'll have a glass of red. Large. Actually, she's my next-door neighbour. She abducted me.'

Bonnie smiled. 'And forced her to dress like a vampire. And I probably shouldn't drink, in case I need to drive later.'

'Car got stuck,' Debbie explained. 'Couple of miles out of the village. You know anyone who could give us a tug?'

'Stuck?'

Bonnie nodded. 'We encountered a herd of cattle and had to pull into the verge. I couldn't get the car back out.'

'Oh dear. And you don't have breakdown coverage? Although, no one would ever find you down here. We're in a GPS blackspot.'

'A what?'

'No phone signals, nothing. It's why it's popular with older folk, and why young people hate it.'

Debbie pulled her smartphone out of her pocket. 'Oh, man. This is going to suck.'

'Where are you ladies heading?' the landlord said. 'Up to Derwent? Or over to Beatrix Potter country?'

Debbie scowled. 'Do I look like I'm into Peter Rabbit?'

'Actually, we're looking for Christmas Land,' Bonnie said. 'The signs all pointed this way, but I'm afraid we seem to have taken a wrong turn somewhere.'

At the mention of Christmas Land, the landlord's countenance darkened. Forcing a smile, he said, 'Well, why don't you ladies take a seat and I'll bring your drinks over. Then we'll come up with a plan of action to get your car out. I'm pretty sure we can figure something out. And after that, I'll see if I can talk you out of going to Christmas Land.'

7

QUIMBECK

THE LANDLORD, WHO INTRODUCED HIMSELF AS LEN Connelly, brought over their drinks. Bonnie lifted an eyebrow at the sight of a large glass of red. The landlord smiled. 'It might take some time to get your car down, but luckily we had a cancellation upstairs for a twin room. Since you were so inconvenienced, I'd be happy to offer you a steep discount.'

'That's very kind of you,' Bonnie said. 'We really must be pressing on to Christmas Land, though. I have to be back at work in a few days.'

The landlord grimaced. 'Well, if you really must go to that hideous place, you can catch a train in the station is at the end of the village. It's the third stop, the one labelled Ings Forest.'

'There's a train?' Debbie asked.

'It's part of the Lake District Heritage Line. Although, the whole line is only five stops, from here in Quim up to Ings Water. The environmentalists shut down any chance of expansion. It's a pretty little thing, although Christmas Land is something we don't like to advertise.'

'Why not?'

Len grimaced. 'It's … unsavoury. Okay, that's putting it lightly. In an area of outstanding natural beauty it's an abomination, everything we're not about: tacky, touristy rubbish. When it opened in the sixties it had a bit of sparkle, but over the years it's fallen nearly to ruin. It only caters to cheap package holiday tourists these days. Stag parties, that kind of thing. The sooner they bulldoze it, the better.'

'It doesn't sound like you're a fan,' Debbie said. Poking a thumb at Bonnie she added, 'You're looking at the proprietor of Mervin's Marshmallow Café.'

Bonnie grimaced. 'An uncle I barely knew left me a hundred year lease in his will. We're going up to take a look.'

'Oh, you're actually staff?'

Bonnie sighed. 'It's more a case of curiosity than anything else. I can't afford to move up here. I imagine this area is pretty exclusive.'

Len nodded. 'There aren't many locals left, and those that are, like myself, are forced into the tourism industry. In here we serve the locals, but all the rest is for the tourists.'

'Well, you have a nice place here.'

'Thank you.'

'Why don't you have a walk around the village after you've finished your drinks?' Len said. 'Just so you can understand why we all dislike Christmas Land so much.'

As Len headed back to the bar, Debbie leaned in to Bonnie. 'Bitter old sod, eh?'

'He seemed very nice.'

Debbie shook his head. 'Nah. Stag parties and all that? Know what they do? Drink beer. And if they're going up to Christmas Land, they're not drinking his.'

'It also means you can get beer up there.'

Debbie grinned. 'A definite plus.'

They took Len's advice and headed out for a walk around the village. Quimbeck was picture-book quaint, all cobble streets, narrow alleyways and tightly clustered stone-walled houses. Among them the river flowed, fish darting about in the clear water, ducks and swans gliding across the surface. They passed several tourists, mostly hikers or elderly couples. A few baulked at the sight of Debbie, but most were quietly polite in their passing greetings, smiling kindly at Bonnie as though sympathetic towards a mother travelling with her rebellious daughter.

They had walked up through the village and had just caught sight of a small train station when Debbie put out a hand, stopping Bonnie in her tracks.

'What is it?'

'Shh. I hear something.'

'What?'

'Be quiet.'

They stood in silence for a few seconds. Bonnie was about to interject again when a voice piped up from inside the station building: 'So, gov'nor, we've got a half hour wait? Anywhere we can get a pint in the meantime?'

Bonnie couldn't hear the reply, but she glanced at Debbie, lifting an eyebrow.

'Is that them?'

As though on cue, three lads appeared out of the station building and strode across the cobblestoned square. The one at the front strutted like something out of a fifties beatnik gang, with the other two hurrying to catch up. Bonnie saw their destination: a newsagent across the street.

'The chavs,' Debbie said. 'This has got to be a bad joke.'

They waited until the three guys had gone into the shop before heading up to the station. From the entrance they could see why Christmas Land was so unpopular in Quimbeck: behind the station was a large car park carefully hidden among trees. A sign announced CHRISTMAS LAND PARKING.

At present there were no more than a dozen cars parked under the trees, but Bonnie guessed that at peak times it could be quite a strain on the local roads to have so many people coming into the village.

Assuming there was a peak time, of course.

Bonnie was still lingering in the waiting area while Debbie went to talk to the station master. Despite the huge car park, there seemed to be little fanfare about Christmas Land here. The decoration inside the station was lots of posters and paintings of various lakes, with a rack of pamphlets advertising local museums, nature walks, boat tours. Christmas Land was conspicuous by its absence.

'Next train is in thirty minutes,' Debbie said. 'Last one of the day. You want to go up?'

Bonnie hesitated, then shook her head. 'We'll wait until the morning,' she said. 'We need to get the car, and anyway … I don't know.'

'Scared of what we're going to find?'

'Something like that.'

'Yeah, doesn't sound appealing, does it?'

They turned for the exit, just as the three lads came in.

At first, all swigging from cans of Carlsberg, they didn't notice the two women. Then the first looked up, stopping so abruptly that the other two knocked into his back.

'Hey guy,' one said, 'Watch your step.'

'Bros, it's the head girl.'

'Merry Christmas,' Debbie said. 'Have you punks been naughty or nice this year?'

The three lads backed up. The first two looked genuinely scared, but the third had a small smile on his lips as though this were part of the entertainment. He was the handsome one, Bonnie decided. The other two were his joker school friends.

'Gonna miss our train,' the first said, backing away onto the platform. 'Come on, lads.'

'Make sure the train misses you too,' Debbie said. 'I haven't eaten yet today.'

As they headed out of sight up the platform, Bonnie laughed. 'You're a natural at this man-eating vampire stuff.'

'Got to keep them in their place.'

'Come on, let's get back to the pub. I'm getting hungry too.'

They headed back down into the village. It was already getting dark, the shadows lengthening across the fells, the first streetlights blinking on. Quimbeck looked even more delightful in twilight, the shadows stretching across the streets, pools of light spilling from bay windows. Even though they had barely been here a couple of hours, Bonnie felt an urge to never leave.

Then, of course, she remembered her mortgage, her rubbish job and even worse salary, and the fact that probably her most valuable possession was a rundown Metro currently stuck in the mud a mile outside the village.

The reality check was like a big, fat slap across the face. People like Debbie and Bonnie didn't live in towns like this. Rich people, people retired on bankers' salaries, stockbrokers with second homes, lawyers seeking a respite from the smoke, they were the people who lived in places like this, not divorced fifty-something checkout staff who had to decide of a month whether she had enough money left out of her salary to buy a new pair of tights.

'Are you all right?'

Bonnie looked up. 'Huh?'

'You look like the singer of your favourite band just died on the eve of a reunion tour. You know what it feels like, don't you?'

'What?'

'To be completely out of place. Sucks, doesn't it?'

Bonnie sighed. 'Yeah.'

'Well, you know what I've learned from experience? The longer you feel it, the less you care. Let's go get your car then find a Benz to park next to.' Debbie grinned. 'And let's not even wash it.'

8

FIRST IMPRESSIONS

THE SUN PEAKING OVER THE FELLS TO THE EAST WAS quite a sight to behold as Quimbeck awakened. With Debbie still sleeping, Bonnie made a cup of tea from the complementary set and sat by the second floor window, watching the dawn sunlight stretching across the town. With the pub set on a slope, she had a view over the village's rooftops to the fells beyond, and the windy lane down which they had come.

Back up the valley, though, was where the most mystery lay. Hidden among the largest stretch of forest in the Lake District, was the semi-mythical Christmas Land.

Today, she would discover her destiny.

On cold winter evenings you can take a sleigh ride through pristine forests, lights back in the trees winking at you, fairies and pixies come out to play. If you're lucky you might see one close up as you journey through the forest to your destination, a simple log cabin in which you'll find a roaring fire, and hot chocolate with marshmallows waiting for you. And there, you can sing Christmas songs as you sit around the fire, and if you're very, very lucky, the door might creak open and a man dressed in red and white might enter, arms laden with gifts for all.

Or she would see her dreams crushed into the dirt.

Leaving Debbie asleep, Bonnie showered, dressed, and ventured downstairs. She found Len waiting for her in the bar, alongside a man who looked vaguely familiar. He introduced himself as Reg Coldsworth, a local farmer.

'Was me cows run you girls off the road yesterday,' he said. 'Least I could do to tow your car. It's outside. Even gave it a hose down.'

Bonnie thanked Reg profusely then hurried outside to check on her Metro. It appeared to have suffered no damage from its night stuck in the mud, so she drove it up to the car park outside the station, then walked back down through the village.

Debbie was up and ready when she got back to the pub, already tucking into a buffet breakfast at a window seat. Bonnie slid in opposite and told her about the car.

'So, we have no more excuses,' Debbie said. 'We're going up to Christmas Land this morning.'

'We are,' Bonnie said.

'Nervous?'

'Terrified.'

Debbie lifted a cup. 'Have a coffee. It's good. Get me a refill on your way up, too, would you?'

'Sure.'

Shortly afterwards, having settled up with Len, who wished them a good trip and told them he expected them back sooner rather than later, they headed for the train station. A chilling November breeze was whipping down through the valley, buffeting Bonnie's hair. Debbie, whose braids were weighed down by ball-bearings, was as unflustered as a ghost marching through the centre of town.

'Still nervous?' Debbie said, as they bought tickets and climbed aboard a quaint steam train waiting at the platform.

'My teeth are practically chattering,' Bonnie said. 'I don't think you understand. I'm realising a childhood dream.'

'To finally find out that Father Christmas is a cardboard cutout, the elves are all drunks, and the reindeer have rabies?'

'It's better than always wondering.'

A whistle blew, and the train chugged out of the station. They were the only passengers. Bonnie looked back wistfully at Quimbeck with its pretty streets and shops. It felt like they were heading off to war.

The valley began to steepen around them, in places the grassy fells becoming craggy and mountainous. The train followed the river, the gurgling waters slowly widening until they crossed over a wooden trestle bridge and then rounded a small lake on their left. To the right, a small hamlet opened out, the stone houses clustered along the lake's edge.

'Merryweather,' called the driver over a loud speaker, and the train came to a stop, a handful of people getting on.

'These villages look all the same after a while,' Debbie said. 'I hope this Christmas Land is going to be a bit different.'

'I could handle living here,' Bonnie said. 'It's the perfect place to meet rich old gentlemen.'

'Nah, you're thinking of the internet,' Debbie said. 'Seriously, if you want to ruin your life with some man we should get you onto some dating sites. I'll vet each potential match, of course.'

'Like a good guardian angel.'

'And anyone who messes you about will get turned into a frog and eaten.'

'I'd hope for nothing less.'

The train pulled away. The next stop, Upwater, appeared to be little more than a jetty with a number of rowing boats moored along its length as it poked out into the water.

'We're next,' Debbie said. 'God, I can hear the sleigh bells already.'

'That's your hair,' Bonnie said.

The train took a sharp right turn, leaving the lake behind and heading into the trees. Thick pine forest rose around them, shutting out most of the light, turning the train line into a virtual tunnel.

'Okay, even I'm getting freaked out,' Debbie said. 'Do you think there are bats?'

'Planning to make friends already?'

Debbie clutched Bonnie's arm. 'Look, I'll let you into a secret. I hate bats. They scare the hell out of me. Don't you know they carry bubonic plague?'

'I hadn't heard that,' Bonnie said. 'But don't worry, it's technically day, so they'll be asleep.'

'But what if the train breaks down?'

'We'll close the window.'

Debbie looked about to hyperventilate. Just as Bonnie was beginning to get worried, the trees opened out. They passed through a boggy section of marshland filled with pretty flowering plants and then pulled into a little station, standing, to all intents and purposes, on its own in the middle of nowhere.

'Ings Forest,' called the driver. 'Passengers for Christmas Land should get off here.'

Bonnie and Debbie climbed off as the train's doors opened. They found themselves standing on a platform lacking even a ticket office. As the train pulled away, chugging across the marsh and then vanishing back into the forest, they looked at each other, both shrugging.

'Well, we're here,' Bonnie said.

'What an awesome place. Like, how long do we have to wait for the next train back?'

'There's a road over there, through the trees. And a sign. Look.'

Carrying their suitcases, they climbed down a set of steps and made their way across the clearing to where a forest trail led into the trees. A faded wooden sign with an arrow said CHRISTMAS LAND THIS WAY.

They headed down the trail, the trees closing in to block out the sky overhead. Debbie clutched Bonnie's arm, squeezing so tightly that Bonnie had to repeatedly prise her fingers free in order to allow the blood to resume flowing.

The trail kept up a winding meander which didn't allow them to see too far ahead, as though holding back its secrets until the last moment. Bonnie was fully expecting to turn a corner and find a sign telling them they'd been duped, when Debbie jerked to a stop, pulling Bonnie with her.

'What happened?'

'Can't you hear it?'

'What?'

'Music.'

Bonnie listened. Debbie was right. A faint tinkle of music came through the trees. It was too indistinct to make out any kind of a tune, but she felt sure it was familiar.

'I don't believe it,' Debbie said. 'Jingle Bells. Don't they know it's November?'

They started walking again. As they closed on the source of the music, Bonnie was able to pick up the tune. Jingle Bells, played on a loop.

'It's so weird,' Bonnie said. 'Standing in a pine forest in November, hearing the most famous Christmas Song of all played over a speaker.'

'Look,' Debbie said. 'Here it is.'

They stepped out from behind a large pine leaning across the path and found Christmas Land standing in front of them.

Huge ornate gates held a sign.

WELCOME TO CHRISTMAS LAND
WHERE THE MAGIC NEVER ENDS

On either side, gatehouse towers rose, all fake stonework and plastic snow. Electric candles flickered in windows, illuminating the silhouettes of reindeer and elves.

One gate stood open. As they approached, Bonnie saw how it was now open forever, the upper hinge broken off, leaving the front corner buried in the ground. Bushes had grown up to claim it, the roots of saplings rooting it into the earth.

Inside the gates were lines of pretty chalets and a visitor centre. The roofs were loaded with pine needles and she could see even from this distance that several windows had plywood boards where glass should have been. A Ferris wheel standing in the centre of a main square had a sycamore growing eight feet high through the window of the closest car to the ground, clearly indicating that it hadn't turned in some years.

'It's derelict,' Debbie said. 'Abandoned. Wow, this is way more awesome than I was expecting. Man, if only I had a metal band, this would be amazing for some press photos. An abandoned Christmas theme park in the middle of the forest—'

'We prefer to simply say neglected,' came a voice from

inside one of the gatehouse towers, and a lower window opened to reveal a ruddy-cheeked man wearing a top hat and a green suit. Large sideburns made Bonnie immediately think of the bankers in *Mary Poppins*.

'While it might look in a little disrepair, I can assure you that there is still plenty of fun to be had in Christmas Land, three hundred and sixty-five days of the year. Do you have a reservation? If not, don't worry. We have plenty of chalets available.' Then, breaking kayfabe for the first time, he looked down at the red gloves covering his hands and grimaced. 'Most of them, actually.'

9

AROUND THE PARK

With Bonnie and Debbie looking on, the man emerged from the gatehouse tower and walked over towards them, nearly tripping once on a piece of cobblestone that had come loose. He paused a few feet away, composed himself, and then performed an elaborate bow, one arm bent across his stomach, the other flailing out behind him.

'Welcome, one and all,' he said, standing up straight again, looking a little flustered as though it wasn't an action he performed very often these days. 'Welcome to Christmas Land, where the magic of Christmas is all year round. My name is Archibald Glockenspiel, but you can just call me Mr. Archie. Mr. Archie, always ready with a song when one is absent. Oh, we wish you a merry Christmas—'

Debbie put up a hand. 'Please stop.'

The man huffed out a sigh and then sagged, bracing himself with his hands on his knees. 'I'm getting a little old for this, I'm afraid.'

'I thought you did it great,' Bonnie said. 'However, I

find it hard to believe that's your real name.'

Archie Glockenspiel laughed. 'Well, aren't you an astute one? You're quite right. My real name is Brendon Jones. Mr. Glockenspiel is for the kids. He turned around, indicating a woodwind instrument pattern on his back. 'If you tap it with a stick it plays a song,' he said, trying to hit himself on the back but finding the costume too restrictive. Debbie stepped up and gave him a tap, wrinkling her nose as an out-of-tune version of *Ding Dong Merrily on High* played for a few notes before petering out.

'I'd better change the batteries,' Brendon said. 'Although these days, the only back slaps I get are from louts on package holidays.'

'I'm afraid we don't have a reservation,' Bonnie said.

'Oh, not to worry, I'll just—'

Bonnie put up a hand. 'I'm Mervin Green's niece,' she said. 'I was sent a letter by his lawyer to inform me that I had been left a lease on his property in his will.'

Brendon's jaw dropped. Beside Bonnie, Debbie sniggered. Brendon looked either about to sink to his knees or break into song.

'Mervin's niece,' he said. 'You came. And even better, you brought your daughter.'

'I'm not her daughter, I'm her best friend,' Debbie said, at the same time that Bonnie said, 'She's not my daughter, she's my best friend.'

'Things will be different now,' Brendon said, his eyes glazing over. 'The Marshmallow Café was always the centre of our park. Without it, things were never the same.' He sighed. 'Mervin … he was such a character.' Then, with a beaming smile, he added, 'And I'm sure you're a chip off the old block. Once the Marshmallow Café is up and running again, I'm certain the park's fortunes will pick up, the glory days will return, and the threat of the bulldozers will finally be vanquished for good.'

Bonnie felt a sudden overwhelming sense of doubt. *I'm a checkout girl*, she wanted to scream. *My husband left me for a woman who sold hats and my children blamed me for not being good enough. My best and only real friend is a Goth vampire half my age. At fifty-two years old the good years of my life are all behind me and there's nothing left to look forward to except getting elderly, sick, and becoming a burden to society*—

'Whatever Martin was, Bonnie here is double,' Debbie said. 'You have no idea. You've just invited a fairy godmother into your midst.'

'As I thought,' Brendon said, beaming.

'His name was Mervin,' Bonnie said. 'Not Martin.' She smiled. 'But I appreciate the vote of confidence.'

'Welcome,' Debbie said. Then, turning to Brendon, she said, 'Mind showing us around a bit? I want to know if there are any night clubs.'

'Certainly,' Brendon said, slipping neatly back into character by executing an extravagant bow. 'Just let me call some elves to take your cases. I'll have them dropped outside the Marshmallow Café. Would that work?'

'Perfect,' Bonnie said.

'Elves?' Debbie added, frowning.

Brendon pulled a bell out of a jacket pocket, held it up, and gave it a sharp shake. At once, three green-clad figures came running out of the other gatehouse's door. Halfway across the gravel, they joined arms, executing a sudden jig somewhere between *Riverdance* and *The Nutcracker*, with a heavy dose of pantomime thrown in. One caught his foot on the same loose cobble that Brendon had, muttered an expletive under his breath that made Debbie snigger, before slipping seamlessly back into step as though such a disturbance was commonplace.

Ending the jig with a neat bow, the three elves rushed forward and picked up the cases Bonnie and Debbie had put down on the ground. At a distance the elves had appeared childlike, but close up, the three were creepily mature, one with a couple of days' worth of stubble, another with a scar alongside his nose. The third had bloodshot eyes as though he spent most nights on the sherry.

'Are they real elves?' Debbie asked, as the three ran off, the two carrying the bags struggling to keep up with the third, who skipped and kicked his legs ups every couple of steps. 'I mean, that's kind of ridiculous, but so is a tumbledown Christmas theme park in the middle of the forest.'

'Gracious, no,' Brendon said. 'Mark, Shaun, and Alan are all aspiring actors, though. They were too old for character parts at Euro Disney, but as you can guess, we're not exactly overrun with staff applications.' He shrugged. 'Talk to any of them in the pub and you'll realise that they're not exactly happy about the circumstances. However, they're professionals, and they do their job as well as could be expected.'

'The middle one looked familiar,' Debbie said.

Brendon nodded. 'Shaun played a car thief on the fourth season of *Casualty*. That's probably where you've seen him.'

Debbie shook her head. 'No, I was thinking he looks like a guy who used to hang around the same job centre as me.'

'Well, he's only been on the staff a couple of months, and he does come from the southwest, so it's possible.'

'It's a small world,' Debbie said, shrugging.

Bonnie lifted an eyebrow. 'Should you be telling us all these insider secrets? After all, we're customers.'

Brendon smiled. 'Well, you're not really customers, are you? You're the new proprietor of the world famous marshmallow café. And more than that, you're both now part of the Christmas Land family. Come with me, let me show you around.' As they started to follow, he added, 'If you don't mind, I'll just slip out of this ridiculous suit into something a little more comfortable. The next train isn't until the afternoon and all the guests are out on organised excursions, so I don't think it'll be necessary. While occasionally we get lost hikers wandering out of the forest, it's not very common.' He winked. 'The bears eat most of them.'

'Is he joking?' Debbie asked, peering suspiciously at the forest around them.

'I hope so,' Bonnie said.

They waited outside the gatehouse while Brendon went inside, emerging a few minutes later in a pair of jeans and a blue jumper.

'Ah, that's better. Right, follow me.'

Behind the main gates, the park opened out into a wide square. Brendon explained how in peak periods it was filled with performers, magicians and acrobats. In winter a stage would be built for a Christmas choir and various bands, and it was the start and end of various parades.

Now it stood empty, populated only by weeds and piles of pine needles blown into clumps and soaked by the rain. Beneath the muck and dirt the remains of a snowflake mosaic was visible, cracked in places, weeds growing through gaps where coloured tiles had broken up.

Several walkways in similar states of disrepair led away from the square. The first of the rides, a merry-go-round, Christmas-themed with reindeer and sleighs instead of horses, stood nearby, a padlocked chain over its entrance.

Debbie wandered over and gave it a shake, then looked up with a frown.

'So, does like, anything run here at all?'

'Oh, there's plenty of life,' Brendon said. 'Several of the shops and bars are open. There is a restaurant forum at the far end of the park, an indoor area where most guests congregate of an evening.'

Bonnie turned to Brendon as he brushed dust off the closed sign of an empty souvenir shop. 'Um, how many customers do you currently have?'

Brendon grimaced. 'Well, including the three young men who showed up yesterday, and yourselves, of course … thirty-five.'

Debbie snorted. 'That's it? No wonder it looks quiet. How many staff are there?'

'Fifty,' Brendon said. Debbie started laughing, only getting control of herself when Bonnie patted her arm. 'At peak periods we used to number around two hundred, but I'm afraid the decline in recent years has meant regular cutbacks. We're a skeleton staff these days, mostly shop and bar staff, cooks and cleaners. We've had to let the maintenance of the place go a little bit, I'm afraid.'

They passed a line of souvenir shops. Three were closed, but lights shone in the windows of the fourth. It was prettily designed with tall, alpine eaves and a Christmas display in the window. A woman in her mid-fifties came to the door and gave them a wave.

'Welcome,' she called in a singsong voice.

'This is June, my wife,' Brendon said. She runs the Wintry Treats Gift Shop, and also Mountain Breeze Snacks and Cakes, across the way there.' He turned to point at a neat café embedded at the end of a line of abandoned ones.

'We're not overrun with customers these days, so I flit

between the two,' she said. 'Have you just arrived? There are some great activities on over the next few days.'

Brendon introduced them both to June. 'Bonnie is Mervin's niece,' he said.

'Oh, how wonderful that you came,' June said. 'Mervin would have been delighted. You will stay with us, won't you?'

'Well, I don't know,' Bonnie said.

'She's pulling a sickie from work,' Debbie said. 'We thought we'd come and take a look at this place.'

'Is that a Krampus costume?' June said, looking Debbie up and down. 'I mean, you need the horns and a mask, plus the basket on your back for the naughty kids….'

Debbie grinned. 'I'm sure it could be adapted.'

'Oh, we're in desperate need of a good pantomime villain,' June said. 'Our last Krampus quit last year. He said there weren't enough people to scare.' Then, turning to Brendon, she said, 'Have you taken them to the marshmallow café yet?'

'Next stop,' Brendon said.

June beamed. 'Wait until you see it,' she said to Bonnie. 'It's wonderful.'

'So I've heard.'

'It's just around the corner,' June said.

They said goodbye to Brendon's wife and made their way down the road, past a stand of trees and another couple of derelict rides, one a water flume ride that currently stood dry, and the other a large warehouse-like building with Snowman's Adventure Maze written in big, bubbly plastic letters over a closed, padlocked door.

'And here we are,' Brendon said, stopping next to a circular fountain, water gurgling weakly from the mouth of a stone angel. He lifted his arms. 'The world famous delight, Mervin's Marshmallow Café.'

Bonnie stared at the building across the plaza, breath catching in her throat. It was everything they had seen in the pictures and more, all towering Elizabethan eaves and latticework windows. In the middle of this tacky, rundown theme park, it was something transported forward through time, a reminder that before the days of prefab plastic and lightning fast construction, architecture had once been beautiful.

She gave a little laugh, like the flutter of a bird. 'I don't know what to say,' she said. 'It's delightful.'

10
THE MARSHMALLOW CAFÉ

THE ELVES HAD LEFT THEIR CASES OUTSIDE THE DOOR. Brendon handed over a key he said Mervin had left with him for safekeeping, then took his leave, promising to stop by later to see how they were getting on.

'Who needs Quimbeck when you've got this?' Debbie said, following Bonnie through the front door into a delightfully antiquated seating area. All around, wooden chairs and tables stood near windows or in partitioned alcoves. Ahead, a serving counter made a gentle arc around the back wall, a wide glass cabinet with metal racks inside, currently empty. An open door behind it led to a kitchen. Through an arch into another seating area that stretched around the side, they found customer toilets and a little play area for children. Unlike the rest of the park, it was spotlessly clean and in immaculate condition.

'What did your uncle die of?' Debbie asked.

Bonnie shook her head. 'The letter didn't say. Perhaps Brendon knows.'

'Where's all his stuff? He lived here, I take it.'

Bonnie shrugged. 'I suppose so. Let's go and take

a look.'

To the side of the kitchen was a door marked PRIVATE. Bonnie opened it, revealing a steep wooden staircase leading up. The electricity was working, a light switch on the wall filling the staircase with a dim, orange glow. Bonnie peered up at another closed door at the top.

She made her way up, Debbie a couple of steps behind. The upper door opened smoothly, revealing a quaint, cottage-like hallway with several closed doors.

'They did take out the corpse, didn't they?' Debbie asked. 'I mean, we don't want any unpleasant surprises.'

'I hope so,' Bonnie answered. 'I think we're about to find out.'

The first room was a guest bedroom, neatly made up with a flowery bedspread and some tasteful Yvgeny Lushpin prints on the walls of Venice, Paris, and San Francisco.

'Bagsy my room,' Debbie said. 'It'll look great once I have a couple of Judas Priest posters up.' At Bonnie's sharp glare, she winked. 'Only joking. I'll do my best to become blandly middle-class for the duration of our stay.'

They found the signs of Mervin's occupation in the other rooms. Bonnie's uncle had lived a sparse life, it seemed. There were a few books and magazines in a bookcase in a pretty living room, and a few personal photographs in frames on a mantelpiece above a fireplace, but Mervin had certainly been no hoarder. Even his kitchen cupboards were mostly empty, as though he had spent most days eating downstairs in the café or out at other restaurants across the park.

The floor above consisted of two more bedrooms, the living room, a small kitchen and a bathroom-toilet. The fixtures and fittings were surprisingly modern compared to the building's exterior, only the wooden eaves reminding

Bonnie that they weren't in some modern townhouse. Mervin hadn't been one for clutter, but he had been one for style; nothing was overstated or out of place. Even Bonnie, who didn't have much of an eye for design, could see how the colours blended and fit, the furniture was appropriate for each room, and the décor was quaint but not imposing. After a long day of hard work, it was the perfect place to sit down and relax with a book.

Bonnie was just about to take a look in the fridge when she noticed Debbie standing by the door.

'What's the matter?'

Debbie grimaced. 'I think this is the personal bit,' she said. 'I'll go take a walk around the park, if that's cool. Leave you to sort through your uncle's stuff.'

'You don't have to—'

'Debbie shook her head. 'It's cool. I want to have a look around anyway.'

'Okay, well, I'll see you in a bit then.'

Debbie smiled. 'If I'm not back by dark, send a search party. I'll likely have been eaten by one of Mr. Glockenspiel's bears.'

Bonnie laughed. 'I hope not. You'd give them indigestion.'

∼

Much as she immediately missed Debbie's incomparable presence, Bonnie appreciated the space. Everything was so difficult to get her head around. Living in a place like this was beyond her wildest dreams. She had got used to a view of a car-choked road and her neighbours' overgrown front yards, but now from her living room she had a view of the plaza with its fountain in the centre, and the shops lining the edge. From the kitchen she could see further up the park, towards the curving tracks of a rollercoaster cutting in and out of the trees. And there, rising high out of the forest was a viewing platform.

Although the electricity worked, the water had been switched off, and it took her a few minutes of poking around downstairs to find a water cut off lever where she could turn it on again. Back upstairs, the taps ran dirty for a few seconds, before the water began to come through clear. Satisfied, Bonnie made herself a cup of tea using some Ahmad English Breakfast teabags she found in a tin. There was no milk, but in a cupboard she found some coffee creamer which was still in date.

Retiring to an armchair in the living room, she sat down with the tea on her lap, gazing at the view outside, wondering whether she had come by an unbelievable stroke of fortune or been lumbered with a burden she didn't need.

Things still didn't seem real. The lawyer's letter had laid out some of the terms that restricted things. She couldn't sell the property, for one. It didn't legally belong to her, although the lease was for an hundred years. Whether that restricted what maintenance she could do on it, she didn't know, but she suspected it was likely. And the biggest question was that if she didn't technically own it, then who did?

Her uncle, like a lot of things in her life, remained a mystery. Had she known he was here all this time, living and working in the middle of a forest in the Lake District, she might have visited. She didn't even know if he had been close to her family, because after her father's death, things had become difficult, with her mother working all hours to keep them afloat. The years of struggle had strained their maternal bond too, and Bonnie's divorce had gained no favours from her elderly mother. Now, at the age of eighty-seven, she lived in a care home in Bristol, and while Bonnie visited as often as she could, during her few moments of clarity, her mother did little other than berate her for seemingly throwing her marriage away.

It remained a sore subject, one she didn't like to think about.

Outside, a wind whipped through the trees, whistling through the eaves and rattling the window. Behind her, something creaked, making Bonnie nearly jump out of the chair. She looked around, and there, in an alcove occupied by a standing lamp, she saw a thin door, no more than two feet wide, cracked open.

Neither she nor Debbie had noticed it. Painted the same dark brown as the rest of the hardwood that elegantly framed the little living room, it had appeared to be part of the paneling, a small notch for a handle only noticeable now as the door caught the light. Debbie stared at it, wondering where it could lead. The dimensions of the house didn't allow for any other rooms on this floor, so perhaps it led to a back stair down to the ground, a fire exit of sorts.

She put her tea aside and got up. She had to move the lamp out of the alcove in order to open the door, but when she cracked it she found a steep hardwood slope leading up, interspersed with ladder-like footholds, something that reminded Bonnie of a ship's hold.

Her fingers tingling with excitement, Bonnie stared up. She hadn't realised that the house had another floor, but now, remembering the design from the outside, it was possible the roof held some kind of attic space.

The stairs opened up on a room that was surprisingly wide, bigger than the living room downstairs but with slanted corners where the roof intersected. Tall enough to stand in, to Bonnie's utter delight, there was yet another door, this one leading outside, up a ladder and onto a rooftop space entirely hidden from the ground. Through a glass window in the door she saw a picnic table and a telescope on a tall stand, angled up to the sky.

It was the attic room which was of most interest, though. Here, she realised, was Uncle Mervin's true living space. Shelves filled with books lined the walls, most of them related to Christmas or festivals. A desk stood against one wall, still heaped with papers and notebooks, as though whomever had discovered Mervin's death had known nothing of this secret personal space.

Without the orderliness of the rooms downstairs, here Mervin's true personality stood out. There were little figurines from all over the world lined on shelves, Russian and Japanese dolls, even, hilariously, a Caganer from Spain in the shape of Margaret Thatcher. And snow globes, too, dozens of them, ornate, expensive ones rather than mass-produced tourist rubbish. In a wicker tray to one side lay piles of letters with postmarks from all over the world, Brazil, Alaska, the Maldives, New Zealand. Some were open, most were still sealed, as though Mervin had died before looking through them. And ringing the desk were several framed photographs, far more personal than the few downstairs.

Bonnie looked at each in turn. One was a picture of a young Mervin with his arms around a woman Bonnie didn't recognise. Now that she thought about it, she didn't know if her uncle had even been married, so perhaps this was some lost love. Another was with a man she recognised with a skip of her heart as her father, their arms around each other's shoulders, a pair of motorbikes standing off to the side, and a lake that was possibly local in the background.

But it was one larger, more prominent photograph

which brought tears to Bonnie's eyes. Inside a thin paper frame with a faded Christmas Land logo along the top, it showed the same two men standing outside the theme park, a freshly decorated gatehouse in the background.

And in the arms of her father, a young girl, no more than three years old.

Bonnie wiped her eyes. She had seen baby photographs of course, and recognised herself immediately.

She had been here before, when the park was new, perhaps before it was even fully opened. Her father had always promised to take her when she was old enough to enjoy it, and now she realised that the stories he had always told her about the park came from personal experience.

They had always felt so real, so clear in her mind that she could almost visualise them. Now she understood why. She had been here before, and locked away in the vaults of her long forgotten memories, were the experiences her father had told her about.

Why he had never told her, she could only speculate. It was unlikely that her mother, perhaps holding the camera in the photograph, perhaps not, would be able to enlighten her, but now she realised that coming here, inheriting Uncle Mervin's legacy, was the closure of a circle that had encompassed her entire life.

Needing something stiffer to drink than a cup of tea before she began the task of sorting through her uncle's things, she descended the stair-ladder, just as she heard Debbie come in downstairs.

They met in the living room. Debbie had a beaming smile on her face and a rosy tint to her cheeks.

'You'll never guess what I found,' Bonnie said.

'Me either,' Debbie answered. 'I have good and bad news. The good is that I found a pub. The bad is that those three lads from yesterday were in it.'

11

NEW FRIENDS

The weight of secrets and revelations hung so heavily on Bonnie that she needed to get out for a while. Debbie offered to show her the pub, so together they walked down a forest path leading among customer chalets and one or two smaller attractions that actually seemed to be open, to the larger restaurant forum area Brendon had mentioned. Inside, a communal seating area belonged to all the encircling restaurants, of which only two restaurants were currently open. Bonnie spotted her first customers—an elderly couple with a Labrador—sitting on a table that overlooked a fish pond.

Here's the pub,' Debbie said, indicating a gloomy, ornate building that looked part ice castle, part dungeon. A sign hung over the door: THE GROTTO: REAL ALES FROM SCANDINAVEA.

Debbie pushed through a heavy wooden door and led them inside. Bonnie blinked, waiting for her eyes to adjust to the gloom. Slowly, an intricately adorned hardwood bar came into focus, then a number of tables and chairs, all of them scored and ancient. The décor looked like a Christmas antiques market had exploded. In one place, the back of a life-sized plastic reindeer appeared to enter one wall, with its front end poking out on the other side. A giant model of an open Christmas present had a giant snow globe poking out, its contents a miniature version of the pub in which they now stood, glitter flakes of sand pushed up through the water by a pump. To Bonnie's delight, goldfish swam between miniature plastic trees.

'Debs!' came a cry from a corner table, and Bonnie looked over to see the three lads they had first encountered yesterday at the service area. 'We got you one in.' Then, on noticing Bonnie, a hail of greetings rose up. 'Hey, Grandma!' 'Mrs. Goggins!' 'We've got you a sherry in. Large!'

'I see you've made your peace with them,' Bonnie said.

Debbie shrugged. 'There were only the four of us here,' she said. 'It was a case of drink with them or have a scrap. I was up for the scrap, but they bought me a pint and decided to make a truce. Plus, see that plastic tub on the bar? Free mince pies. Who could possibly stay angry in such a situation? It is Christmas after all, kind of.' She grinned. 'They're all right, for a bunch of chavs. Come on, I'll introduce you.'

She led Bonnie over to the table.

'All right?'

'Get on.'

Debbie planted Bonnie on a chair beside her, facing the three lads. From a distance they had been indistinguishable, but up close they separated into three clearly different beings. The first, introduced as Larry, was short, chunky and prematurely balding, yet had the kind of cherubic face which was likely asked for I.D. whenever he ordered a drink. He was the loudest of the three, the origin of most of the jibes, something Bonnie suspected was due to a secret inferiority complex.

The second, Barry, was harmless in a banker's son kind of way. He was the kind of person destined to progress through life with little fuss, securing a decent job and a pleasant family along the way. His hair parted centrally in an unfashionable throwback to 1990s boybands, and while he was nice enough looking, he wasn't the sort of person to turn many heads. It turned out that he was due to get married soon, and this trip was his stag weekend, booked and organised by his two best friends since primary school.

It was immediately apparent why Debbie had cast off her anger and made peace with them. The third guy, Mitchell, had something about him that the others lacked. He was dark-haired, olive-skinned, and had the kind of brooding look which made girls stumble. Bonnie, long out of the social loop, was able to view as an outsider the way Debbie offered all of her attention to everything Mitchell said, sitting with her body open to him in a subconscious gesture of welcoming. It was sweet in way, although she feared that Debbie, dressed in leathers and chains and with an obsession with Ozzie Osborne, was setting herself up for a fall. Mitchell, all Ralph Lauren and Burberry, his shoes some posh Italian brand they definitely didn't sell in Morrico, was about as opposite as a person could get.

'So, you just got a letter telling you that you'd inherited a café in this place?' Larry said, as conversation turned to Bonnie. 'Mental.'

Bonnie shrugged, wondering how much Debbie had told them. 'It was a surprise, that's for sure.'

'What are you gonna do, like, jack your job in and move up here?'

'I haven't decided yet. It doesn't look as though it would be that lucrative.'

'We'd all stop in for a hot chocolate with marshmallows,' Barry said. 'Wouldn't we, boys?'

'Yeah, course,' Larry said. 'There's only that other café open and that hot chocolate's milk was definitely off.'

'It was goat's milk, you idiot,' Barry said. 'Plus, Mitchell topped you up with some bourbon while you were in the toilet.'

Mitchell, quieter than the others, just smiled as Larry turned to glare at him.

'I wouldn't get your hopes up,' Bonnie said. 'I'm not sure I could open it any time soon.'

'Ah, sucks. Not much else going on up here. Know what we did this afternoon? Elf hunt in the forest. Mental. They got these wolves to pull us on these sleds which had wheels because there ain't no snow—'

'Huskies,' Barry said. 'They weren't wolves.'

'Looked like wolves.'

'That's because they're actual Siberian huskies, not the bred down ones you see middle-aged women walking on Saturday afternoons.'

Larry shrugged. 'Reckon they were close enough. We had to like, drive around, looking for people dressed in elf costumes. If you spotted more than five, you got a prize. Turned out to be a box of out-of-date Christmas crackers. Wasn't hard, though. Found one of them having a cig round the back of this old shed that was supposed to be where they put the reindeer.'

Debbie gave a loud laugh, immediately cutting it off and glancing at Mitchell. 'He was having a cig?'

'Yeah, mental ain't it?'

'I don't think they take their jobs too seriously,' Barry said. 'I mean, it must be hard when there's no one here.'

'Not Christmas yet, is it? I bet it gets packed in December. You reckon they open up those rides? I spoke to that caretaker guy we saw and he was like, no chance. He said that coaster ain't gone in years. Costs too much to run it when there ain't no one on it.'

'Beers are good,' Barry said, lifting a nearly empty glass. 'Who's for another?'

Even though Bonnie was keen to get back and start sorting through Uncle Mervin's belongings, she let them talk her into another drink. As their conversation shifted to other things, she began to feel a little sidelined, and it wasn't just that she was double their age. While they lamented the fall of the once-great park, all she could see in her head was how her father had described it.

And after a long, hard day of trekking through the snow, out to the ice lake in the forest where you can skate in winter and watch rare birds in summer, it's back to the forum, where a great vat of steaming hot chocolate, along with a mound of freshly baked marshmallows, is waiting. Christmas songs are playing, reindeer are wandering past the windows, and a light snow is falling. You're in heaven.

It wouldn't take much to put it right, would it? A decent clean up, a little maintenance, and some better advertising. Leaflets through doors, ads online. Wasn't that how Morrico did it. And that place was always packed.

The five of them enjoyed another drink together, then decided to head out. The boys were only staying until Thursday, doing a mid-weeker because, as Larry told Bonnie in an aside when Barry couldn't overhear, 'It was dirt cheap, like they practically paid us to come.' Before parting, the boys invited Bonnie and Debbie to meet them for dinner, in one of the few open restaurants, a place standing just up the walkway from the forum called Twinkle Star's Christmas Grill.

'Apparently the steaks are the best in the Lake District,' Larry said. 'So fresh you can practically hear the cow mooing.'

Bonnie grimaced at the thought, but Larry meant well. While Debbie instantly agreed, Bonnie was more conservative, telling them she would feel how her ancient bones were holding up a little later on. As they walked back to the café, arm in arm, she wanted to tell Debbie about the secret grotto they had found, but the minute the boys were out of sight, Debbie turned to Bonnie, her cheeks flushed, her eyes practically bobbing out of her head.

'Oh my god,' she said. 'What am I going to do?'

Bonnie smiled. 'What's the problem?'

'It's Mitchell,' Debbie said, the earnestness in her voice making Bonnie laugh. 'I think I'm in love.'

12

STAFF QUARTERS

Debbie was keen to wax lyrical about a man she'd known less than two hours, but Bonnie suggested they wait until they got back to the café and tried to find something less mood-enhancing to drink. In the end, she sat Debbie down in the café's upstairs living room and made some coffee out of a jar Mervin had left behind.

'He doesn't speak,' Bonnie said, handing Debbie a cup.

'Oh, but isn't that part of the mystery? It's like, he could be anything.'

'You're hoping he's actually a guitar player in a metal band, but he's probably an accounts manager at Lloyds.'

Debbie grinned. 'You know me so well. Let's hope on that guitar player thing. He can't have much money if this was where they came for a stag do. Hardly a weekend in Prague, is it?'

Bonnie patted her on the arm. 'You keep your dreams alive as long as you can. Because once you marry one, you'll find out that most men are like radiation. When exposed to real life they immediately begin to deteriorate.'

'Your old man can't have been all bad. I mean, you must have had some good times, right?'

Bonnie gave a wistful smile. 'It was all right in the beginning, I suppose. He was just a player. I knew it when I married him, and he didn't change. I thought he would, but … nope. The problem with being young is that more often than not, you marry for looks. Someone a bit nice shows some interest in you, and you overlook the little niggles and imperfections because they have a nice smile or they touch you in a way that makes you shiver. Ten years in, though, and that's all gone. The rot has set in. If you don't have that meeting of personalities, you're done for. Sure, Phil stuck around for the sake of the kids, but I knew they weren't business trips. And eventually, when the kids were old enough to fend for themselves, he went off on one and didn't come back.'

'That's sad.'

'It is, but is pretending any sadder? I knew for years what he was doing. You can just tell by the body language when they no longer have any interest in you. Don't get me wrong, though, I wouldn't have been any kind of a saint given half the chance. It was just that no one was ever looking at me.'

'Stop. You're going to make me cry. Usually it takes at least five beers, but I think we're at a higher altitude.'

'All I'm saying is to be careful of the holiday romance. Or if you do have one, treat it as that and don't be broken-hearted if it goes nowhere.'

'So you don't think I should try to pull him at the club tonight?'

'The club?' Bonnie grinned. 'I didn't get an invite to that.'

Debbie looked pained. 'It must have come up while

you were in the bog. It's only the cellar underneath the pub. They have a dancefloor.'

Bonnie laughed. 'You have a good time.'

'I'll try. At least I'll have your shoulder to cry on if things go tits up. So, what are you going to do about this café?'

Bonnie let out a slow breath. She had been avoiding the question herself, but now that Debbie had brought it up again, she knew she had to face it. And soon: she couldn't blag a second week off work. It was go back to the smoke and her old life, or give it up and take up residence as a hermit in the middle of a mostly abandoned theme park.

'You'd think, wouldn't you, that this would be like a dream come true,' she said. 'I mean, it would for most people. The thing is, I don't know the first thing about running a café. All I know about marshmallows is how to scan them at the till and burn them over a barbeque. I'd be hopeless. And for all I know, the park could be gone in a couple of years anyway. Then where would I be?'

'You know, your house might not be all that to look at, but you could get a solid rent on it from someone from London,' Debbie said. 'They love that whole seafront life.'

'I don't live anywhere near the seafront,' Bonnie said.

'You could walk it,' Debbie said. 'Technically.'

'In about half an hour, if you pushed it. And Weston isn't exactly the Costa del Sol.'

Debbie rolled her eyes. 'L.O.L. at the ninties ref,' she said. 'And anyway, it's retro. People love that these days.'

'This place is retro,' Bonnie said. 'And it's deserted.'

'That's only because no one knows it's here.'

Bonnie frowned. 'No, I suppose you're right.'

In the end, Bonnie decided to skip out of dinner and whatever Christmas Land considered clubbing and have a quiet night. She cleaned and tidied Mervin's flat—even though she knew she had to start referring to it as her flat—made up Debbie's bed with fresh sheets from an airing cupboard, then began the arduous task of getting the place organised.

She decided to leave the attic grotto until the morning. Luckily, Mervin had kept everything personal in the one place, so the downstairs area just needed a sort and a clean. It appeared he had died several months before the letter arrived, and the house had been left untouched. Everything fresh was now long gone off, both in the flat's cupboards and those in the café downstairs. She was lucky to find a roll of bin liners in a drawer next to the sink, but by the time she was finished, half of them were full. She lined them up inside the café's front door, afraid if she left them outside some animal would come and rip them open.

While she still hadn't decided what to do, she quickly realised she needed more information from someone. She had no idea where the nearest supermarket was nor how to get there, nor when rubbish was collected, where the collection points were, whether she had to sort recycling or not, and whether it was collected on the same day or different. It was a logistic nightmare she had just a few short days to figure out, so after eating a quick dinner of spaghetti with some meat sauce which was only a week past its sell-by date, she headed outside, hoping to find Brendon still on duty.

She hadn't noticed nightfall, but as she stepped outside of the café's front door, her breath caught in her throat. Lights had come on all over the park. Ornate lamp posts stood on every walkway corner and strings of lights hung in the trees. Patches of darkness showed where some bulbs needed to be replaced, but even in its obvious state of disrepair, and lacking any of the snow which would make it truly magical, the effect was enchanting. Bonnie, marvelling at the scene, locked up the café and zipped her jacket shut. Then, hearing the tinkle of classical music coming from hidden speakers, she headed for the park's entrance.

She was nearly there when a dark shadow stepped out from behind a closed shop, startling her. For a moment she stood motionless as the creature, standing to her shoulder, turned in her direction, snorted, and then moved off. A moment later a second followed it, followed shortly after by a tiny version, hurrying to keep up, hooves clacking on the paving stones.

Reindeer. Bonnie couldn't remember ever seeing one this close, but as they moved off across the park, picking at patches of grass, she felt a shiver run up her arms, and she shook her head in disbelief.

She was just about to head off when a figure stepped out from the same shadows. Dressed in green, she recognised Mark, the stubbly-faced elf character from before.

'Oh, hey,' he said. 'Should I stick to character or is it okay to dress down?'

'You're good,' Bonnie said. 'Where are they going?'

'Hopefully back to the stables,' Mark said. 'We lock them up at night otherwise they'd eat all the greenery. We let them roam in winter, if it snows. I've got the rest inside, but these three had wandered over near the gates.'

'Are they wild?'

He shook his head. 'I've only been here a couple of years, but they're brought up tame. If the park was busier we'd probably keep better tabs on them, but some of the fences of their enclosure need a bit of work done and the deer have a habit of getting out and wandering off. As long as people keep their dogs on leads, there shouldn't be any problems.'

Bonnie remembered the Labrador she had seen. 'I suppose that's for the best.'

'Certainly is. They look harmless, but those antlers would toss a dog into the lowest tree branches.' He laughed. 'So, how are you setting in? I heard from Brendon that you're taking over the Marshmallow Café.'

'I haven't decided what to do,' Bonnie said.

Mark nodded. 'So much potential,' he said. 'But this place needs a collective kick up the butt, and a fresh injection of enthusiasm. I heard it used to be amazing, fifty years ago.'

'I heard the same. What happened?'

'People got bored, moved on to different things. And the park stayed the same. You've got to move with the times, or you're done for. All the shop owners got old and retired or died, and no one wanted to take over. The usual thing. It's only still open because the big dog is bankrolling it out of his pocket.'

'The big dog?'

'The boss. The owner. No one's quite sure who it is, but he's clearly pretty loaded. Word has it he's about run out of patience now.'

'The park does appear a little … neglected.'

'It's running at less than a quarter of full operation,' Mark said. 'More rides closed than open. While a few of them are rusted solid, most just need a good oiling and they'd be off again. No staff, no customers … it all adds up eventually to no park.'

Bonnie nodded. 'Do you know where Brendon is? It's some of this stuff I need to talk to him about.'

'Yeah, he's over in the staff briefing room. You know it?'

'No idea.'

'I'll take you there. The park officially closes to new visitors half an hour after the last train. All day staff then report for a debrief.'

'If I opened the café, would I have to attend?'

Mark smiled. 'No, as a leaseholder you'd go to the leaseholders' meetings. Different system, because even though we're all involved, leaseholder businesses aren't part of the main park.'

'Not sure I understand.'

'Kind of like a contractor. You pay a percentage to the park but the rest is yours. Most of the current onsite shops are leaseheld, which is why the park itself is broke. And they're only making money because there's so little competition. I think you'd better get a lowdown from Brendon. I'm just an old man in an elf suit. For what it's worth though, we're all hoping you stay. In the couple of years I've been here, Mervin's was the place to go. What he put in those marshmallows, I'll never know, but they tasted heavenly.'

'Thanks. I'll do what I can.'

Mark led her to the main square and indicated a door between two closed tourist shops. Light glowed through frosted glass over the door. As Mark bid her goodnight and hurried off in pursuit of the reindeer, Bonnie wondered if she was subconsciously talking herself into giving the café a go. There was so much to consider. The lease meant that the land beneath the cottage could be sold out from under her at any time, and while Bonnie knew little about housing legality other than that her mortgage was far higher than it ought to be, it couldn't be good. The park could close around her, leaving her sitting in a customerless café in the middle of a forest.

And not to mention that to open it, she would have to somehow figure out how to run it. Mervin had been here for fifty-odd years; Bonnie less than a day.

She gave the door a polite knock, then tried the handle. It opened quietly on to a narrow corridor with none of the ornate decoration of the shop fronts. Down the corridor Bonnie found herself in the lobby of what looked like a convention centre, doorways leading off into rooms of chairs and fold-out tables all pointing at whiteboards or projector screens.

To the left she heard voices. She walked down the corridor until she heard sound behind one of the doors. She gave a light knock and then opened the door.

About thirty people, many of them dressed in elaborate Christmas-themed costumes, turned to look at her. Behind them, standing by a blackboard covered with numbers and red, downward-pointing arrows, was Brendon.

'I do apologise,' Bonnie said. 'I don't suppose I could come in? I'm afraid I'm still trying to figure things out about this place.'

13

DECISIONS AND DILEMMAS

Brendon came over with three cups of hot chocolate on a tray. After sitting through the end of a depressing meeting about declining park performance, the staff had been dismissed and Bonnie found herself alone with Brendon and his wife June. Brendon led them through into a dated but more comfortable room where they took an armchair each around a coffee table. Bland, strip lights made everything clinical; not even a dusty piece of tinsel hanging over the door was able to lift the sombre mood.

'My boss thinks I have the flu,' Bonnie said. 'I can get away with being off work until the weekend, but by next Monday I really need to know if I'm going back to work or not. I'm not in a position where I can go a long period unemployed, and it looks like there would be quite a lot of risk involved in coming here.'

June and Brendon exchanged a glance. Bonnie could tell it wasn't the opening statement they had been hoping for.

'Mervin's Marshmallow café used to be a central hub of the whole park,' June said. 'Lots of people came just because of it, especially during the off-season, when he would prepare seasonal varieties of marshmallows. Your uncle was a culinary artist when it came to them.'

Bonnie grimaced. 'That's what I was afraid of. The only thing I know about marshmallows is how to open a packet. There can't be much to it, surely?'

'Mervin's were homemade,' Brendon said. 'From natural products, traditional recipes. That area of marsh behind the Ings Forest station was where he sourced his mallow plants from.'

'Mallow plants? I thought marshmallows were made with gelatin.'

June laughed. 'Now they are, but not in ancient Egyptian times.'

'You're joking, aren't you?'

June shook her head. 'Mervin made his marshmallows according to ancient recipes and methods. It's why his café was so famous. He sold types of marshmallows you can't buy anywhere else, at least not in England.'

Bonnie leaned back on the chair, feeling a growing sense of inadequacy. 'I could never do that.'

'You don't know unless you try,' Brendon said. 'It would really help the park if you stayed.'

'How can I know if the park will be here much longer?'

Brendon sighed. 'You don't. None of us do. Things are up in the air right now. The local authority is considering closing the train line, meaning we'd be cut off. There is another access road, but it runs over private land and the terms of usage are for commercial deliveries only. It can't be used for customers.'

'So no one will be able to get in?'

'Like everything else, they have to make a profit, and this branch of the railway was originally built to service our customers. Without any, it's obsolete.'

'But why would any customers want to come all the way across the country to a park where nothing works and most of the shops are shut? You can see wandering reindeer at pretty much every farm park nowadays.'

Brendon nodded. 'That's half the problem.'

'Well, can't we—I mean, you—switch on a few more rides?'

'Without the customers, they won't make any money.'

'And without the rides, you won't have many customers.'

Brendon spread his hands. 'You see what I mean?'

'Christmas Land was built on the personalities and uniqueness of its leasehold businesses,' June said. 'Matilda's Twirl Cakes, the Lonely Pine Steakhouse, the Evening Shadow Cookie Stop, Mervin's Marshmallow Café … they gave the park a feel guests couldn't get anywhere else. And now they're almost all gone.'

Bonnie stood up. 'I didn't ask for any of this,' she said. 'Two days ago I was checkout person at Morrico, and I don't think anything has happened to change that. It's been a nice idea, and I've enjoyed the experience immensely, but I don't think I can make such a difference. I'm a no one. I'm used to being a no one, and I can't think how all this could change me. I'd only disappoint you all if I tried. I'm sorry.'

She ran for the door, not giving them a chance to talk her around. It was a stupid idea, thinking she could turn herself from a faceless checkout person to the proprietress of a world famous café overnight, and somehow not be an utter fraud. Perhaps her children were right: it had been her fault that her husband had run off. After all, who was she really? A no one. She could be erased from existence tomorrow and no one would notice.

No one, perhaps, except the black-clad girl standing

outside the café door when she got back, swaying from side to side, banging on the door and weakly shouting up at the windows for Bonnie, as though afraid of waking anyone up. Bonnie glanced at her watch and was surprised to see it was nearly midnight. The time had flown by.

'Debbie? What on earth are you doing?'

'I don't have a key.'

Bonnie laughed. 'The door's not locked.'

'Yes it is.'

'That's because this is the back door, not the front door, which I told you I would leave unlocked.'

'Oh.'

Debbie swayed drunkenly from side to side. Bonnie smiled, reminded of the first time they had met. 'Come on, follow me. Did you have a good night?'

Debbie grinned. 'The best. This place is awesome. It was metal night. Christmas songs covered by metal bands. I've never been rocked so hard. The lads … oh, the lads, they had no idea what hit them.'

'They enjoyed it?'

'We borrowed some scissors from behind the bar and rocked up their clothes a bit.'

'You cut up their clothes?'

'We did it together. It was awesome. They're like my best mates now.'

'Oh, thanks.'

'But not as best as you. You're the ultra best. The double best.'

'That's great.'

'We have to stay here forever, and become elves or something. Heavy metal elves. That's the best thing ever. Playing guitar from the back of a reindeer. Nothing could ever rock harder. Nothing.'

'Sounds nice.'

She led Debbie inside. As soon as they were out of the cold, Debbie's legs sagged. Afraid she was going to pass out right there on the café floor, Bonnie guided her up the stairs and into the spare bedroom. Debbie slumped down on the bed, snoring almost before she hit the pillow. Bonnie, fondly remembering the first few times her daughter and son had met alcohol, did her best to make Debbie comfortable, painstakingly unlacing and pulling off Debbie's boots, then her coat, and then finally putting a blanket over her. With a smile, she turned out the light and shut the door.

By the time Debbie was settled, it was half past twelve, but Bonnie felt too wired to sleep. She went to the kitchen, poured herself a glass of wine out of a bottle from a rack next to Mervin's old microwave, then headed up through the secret door to Mervin's grotto. From there, she took the door leading up to the rooftop balcony.

With a coat wrapped around her, the temperature was just about bearable, but the view made every second worth it. The park's lights were still on, lines of Christmas lights stretching away into the trees. Overhead though, the sky was clear, and looking up, she saw a sea of stars in all directions.

Could she be happy here? Could this be her life, the owner of a café in the middle of a theme park she had dreamed about since she was a child?

She shook her head. At fifty-two, that stargazing child was a long way behind her, almost forgotten. The reality of Christmas Land, a child's dream, was far more difficult. It was sales figures and accounting and customer access and recipes. Yet, it was also beauty, and friendship, and seeing the delight on a person's face as their day was made. When had anyone she served at Morrico ever looked like they were happy to be there? There were the shrugs and tired smiles, the frustration, the guarded eyes, the stress as some kid played up, as some item was forgotten, as a card transaction failed, as a bag inadvertently split.

She sighed, sipping her wine, then allowed herself a brief smile. It was a stroke of luck that she was even here. It might not work out, but the Old Ragtag thought she had flu; she was good for the next few days.

It wouldn't hurt to give herself until the end of the week.

14

JINGLE BELLS

Just the sight of Debbie in the kitchen, humming some rock track as she prepared breakfast, seemingly unaffected by whatever she had drunk last night, made Bonnie feel hungover. She guessed a late night and a single glass of wine equaled a rough night for someone of fifty-two.

'All right?' Debbie said, noticing Bonnie. 'What happened? You get on the lash with those elves?'

'What elves?'

'Bumped into Mark, Shaun and Alan in the club last night. Mark said he saw you wandering about.'

Bonnie shook her head. 'No, he just gave me directions.'

'Cool bunch of guys. Drink like fish.' Debbie laughed as she poured coffee and handed Bonnie a cup. 'You coming out today, or do you have to do admin and stuff?'

'Coming out?'

'Well, we're kind of on holiday, aren't we? The lads are going on a sleigh ride this morning. Said we should come along.'

Bonnie smiled. 'Sounds great. I'll need some food in me first.'

'Cool. Get ready and we'll head out to that other café. Maybe you can get us a park staff discount.'

'We'll see.'

~

Debbie's enthusiasm was infectious. By the time they were walking across the park to the Mountain Breeze Snacks and Cakes Café, Bonnie felt a spring in her step. She needed to sort through Mervin's stuff, but it wouldn't hurt to have a little fun first.

The café was empty, but it buzzed with order and life in comparison to the closed, bolted, and weed-attacked properties around it. June was nowhere to be seen, a lad in his late teens behind the counter. His glasses glittered with tinsel and he wore a Christmas hat over unruly blond hair.

'Hey Debs,' he said as they entered. Bonnie glanced at her, mouthing, 'Do you know everyone?'

'All right, Niall. Sorry I threw that beer over you last night.'

The boy grinned. 'No probs. You get back okay?'

'Yeah, more or less.'

Bonnie decided not to ask how they had met. 'Do you do breakfasts?' she asked.

'Course.' Niall smiled and handed over a menu. It was a simple piece of paper fitted into a foldout spell-book-shaped holder, a quaint touch. 'You must be Mervin's niece, right?' He reached over a hand for her to shake. 'Lovely to meet you. He was a great old guy. Always slipped me an extra marshmallow, and his cooking classes were awesome.'

'Cooking classes?'

'Yeah. He used to show us traditional cooking methods using natural ingredients. Will you be starting those up again?'

'I can show you how to start a microwave.'

Niall laughed as though it was the funniest joke in the world, but Debbie shot Bonnie a savage glare. Bonnie, wondering quite what she'd done wrong, looked down at the menu.

'Um, I'll just have a reindeer toast set,' she said. 'Whatever that is.'

'Toast shaped like reindeer with jam made in Lapland,' Niall said.

'They have fruit in Lapland?'

'I have no idea, but it's a popular set with the kids. Even more since Frozen came out. We're not allowed to name the characters due to copyright issues, but the kids all know.'

'Popular with kids? Um—'

'And adults.'

Bonnie smiled. 'All right, I'll take it.'

'And I'll have a triple sausage and egg goat-herder's burger set,' Debbie said. She glanced at Bonnie. 'Since we're on holiday and all.'

'Great,' Niall said. 'Shall I charge it to Mervin's account?'

'His account?'

'Yep. All the leaseholders have one.'

'Well, when do I have to settle it?'

'When the lease runs out.'

'So … at the end of a hundred years from the start of the lease?'

'That's right.'

Bonnie laughed. 'Well, in that case, I'll have a large coffee too.'

'And I'll have a larger one,' Debbie said. 'With extra coffee in it.'

Niall clicked his fingers. 'I'll see what I can do.'

As they took a corner table, Bonnie turned to Debbie. 'What was all that about with glaring at me?'

Debbie scowled. 'You're not getting it yet, are you? I've been wandering around the park, talking to staff and customers, and us being here—well, mostly you, but you know, they're loving my get up—has created a real buzz. It seems like your Uncle Mervin was a total legend, like he kept the park's light burning when it was trying to go out. When he died last summer, all the hope that this park could be revived died with him. Then, when we showed up yesterday … it was like Father Christmas had come early.'

'That's a load of rubbish.'

'Look, pack it in with the negativity. There are people here who've worked here almost as long as your uncle did. You showing up has given them a reason to dream.'

Bonnie rubbed her eyes. 'I'm a fifty-two-year-old divorced checkout lady from Weston super Mare. I'm about as far from any kind of hope they could get.'

Debbie shook her head. 'Oh, you poor delusional thing. Here, you're none of that. You're the niece of Christmas Land's most famous resident. You're the park's only hope.'

'Are you quoting Star Wars?'

Debbie grinned. 'Not closely enough to get sued. Come on, snap out of it.'

Bonnie sighed. 'I'll try.'

'Food's up,' came Niall's cheerful voice. As he put two plates down in front of them, Bonnie stared. While her own reindeer shaped toast, complete with icing sugar and a dollop of dark orange apricot jam, was impressive enough, Debbie's tower stack was like something out of a meat factory nightmare. Debbie grinned at the leaning tower of heart disease, as sauces in various colours dripped down on to her plate.

'That'll sort me out,' she said.

∼

After a pleasant walk along nearly deserted tree-lined avenues, past a number of closed shops and attractions, they came to the reindeer stables. Larry, Barry, and Mitchell were waiting on a bench outside, eating donuts and drinking milkshakes from cups shaped like Christmas tree ornaments. Larry looked puffy and red as though he'd run here, and Mitchell looked as sultry as he had yesterday, but Barry was ashen, his eyes drooping. Bonnie wondered how he was handling the stag holiday.

'He all right?' Debbie asked.

Larry grinned. 'Couldn't find anywhere selling Red Bull,' he said. 'Pub's not open until twelve. Reckon a good sleigh ride'll sort him out.'

'I feel sick,' Barry said.

A bearded man in overalls appeared out of the nearest stable and clapped his hands together. 'Good morning, everyone,' he said. 'My name's Jason, and I'll be your driver for today. I'm just getting the sleigh hooked up, and we'll be ready to go in a couple of minutes.'

'Come on, Baz, on your feet, lad,' Larry said, clapping his friend on the shoulder.

Shakily, Barry stood up. 'Might as well die standing,' he said. 'I'll stand at the back, just in case.'

As the others all grimaced, the jingling of bells rose up from the stall behind them. Wooden doors swung wide and four reindeer trotted into view, pulling a beautiful brass-framed sleigh.

'Oh wow,' Debbie said.

Bonnie was too stunned to say anything. The swirling patterns of the metal and the way the sunlight through the trees glinted off it, Bonnie felt like she had stepped through a portal into a fairytale world. The reindeer, with bells hung from their harnesses, jingled as they stamped and snorted. Jason, now dressed in dark green forest garb like a latter day Robin Hood, gave an elaborate bow.

'Welcome to the Christmas Land sleigh adventure,' he said. 'Let's get you settled and then we'll begin our journey.' With a wink he added, 'One of the perks of not being busy is you get the full, uncensored tour.'

They climbed in, the three lads taking a rear bench, with Bonnie and Debbie in front. Jason sat in a seat ahead of them, the reins in his hands. He gave them a shake and the reindeer moved ahead with a sudden jolt, bringing a cry of delight from everyone except Barry, who groaned. The sleigh, fitted with wheeled runners in the absence of any snow, followed a leafy path through the trees, ducking under walkways and angling around lines of chalets and clusters of shops. They waved whenever they saw anyone, but the park was eerily empty.

After a couple of minutes of following beneath the rusting curve of the rollercoaster dipping down above them and then cutting back up through the trees, they came to a tall fence. A gate was set into it. Jason climbed down and opened it, then moved the sleigh forward into a fenced box with another gate at the other end. He got down again, closed the first gate, and then opened the second, before leading them out into the forest outside the park. Pausing once again, he got down and closed the second gate.

'What you got an airlock for?' Larry asked.

Jason glanced back, smiling. 'Now the tour really

begins,' he said. 'Before we were just getting out of the park. Now we're out into the open forest, and who knows what we might find?'

'Bro, don't scare us. You got bears out here or something?'

Jason laughed. 'Actually, yes.' To a series of exclamations, he explained, 'We're now in a nature reserve owned by Christmas Land. Organised walks and tours only. There are a couple of bears, but you don't need to worry. They're European black bears, weighing around a hundred kilograms, and they generally won't attack people.'

'So, by "generally won't", you mean, they sometimes do?' Debbie asked, leaning forward. 'Instead of going on a pretty forest sleigh ride we could actually get savaged by a bear?' She started rummaging in her pockets. 'I hope I've got my phone….'

Jason laughed again. 'No one has ever been attacked in here. In fact, the bears are pretty shy. They won't come near, if we see them at all.'

'Just bears?'

Jason shook his head. 'No, there are wolves. And a few other animals that used to be commonplace in the British Isles but have long since been hunted into extinction. This place is so unique that it's not even shown on most maps. Generally, only researchers and scientists come here. It's only being used for sleigh rides because the park is so quiet. When we're busy, most rides are just around the perimeter.'

'I'm going to be sick,' Barry said, as the sleigh started off, bumping along a forest track, ferns and bushes whipping at the sleigh's sides as they cut between trees. Bonnie stared at the forest as it spread out around them, towering oaks and sycamores, ash and beech. As they briefly rose over a bowl, she caught a glimpse of several rabbits hopping through the trees. And then it came, echoing through the forest: a howl.

'Oh my,' Larry said. Bonnie glanced back to see him cup a hand over his mouth. 'I totally like needed to swear then, but I held it in. We're going to die, aren't we?'

'It's all part of the fun,' Jason said. 'See if you can spot them. We're coming up to a clearing where you can usually see one or two.'

The sleigh rattled through the trees, bumping over rocks. Jason, clearing enjoying himself, made regular jokes about wheels falling off and having to walk back. Debbie clutched Bonnie's arm like a life buoy, while in the back, Barry and Larry made groans of discomfort and nervous grumbles. Mitchell said nothing, but his darting eyes revealed his unease.

Bonnie, however, had settled into the ride and was enjoying it more with each passing moment. The feel of clean forest air on her face, the call of the birds, even when she had to duck sharply to avoid a branch swinging for her face, it all made her feel more invigorated. The feel of wind in her hair, the grunts of the reindeer and the creak of the sleigh … nothing else felt quite like it. No wonder Mervin had stayed all these years.

Finally, Jason steered them between two trees and a fence appeared up ahead. To Bonnie's surprise she realised they had arrived back at the park. As Jason climbed down to open up the gates, he turned back and gave them a wistful smile.

'Didn't see the wolves or the bears, I'm afraid. Maybe next time. I hope you all had a good ride.'

A few minutes later, they pulled up outside the stables, where they found a group of older people waiting in line for the next ride. Barry, who had managed to survive the ride without being sick, looked much better than he had when they set out. Mitchell, brushing a strand of hair out of his eyes, climbed down with the ease and grace of a movie star getting out of a limousine. He held out a hand to Debbie, and Bonnie noticed black painted fingernails. She smiled as she watched Debbie take his hand and climb down; perhaps there was some connection between them after all.

'Right then,' Larry said, clapping his hands together. 'That was awesome. What's even more awesome is to celebrate our survival with a pint.'

Barry and Debbie cheered. Bonnie noticed how Debbie and Mitchell were still holding hands. She smiled. The strangest things could bring young lovers together. As they all headed off in the direction of the pub, she wondered when would be best to slip away.

She had work to do.

15

COMING AROUND

After a quick, social glass of sherry, Bonnie played the old person card and left the others to make merry. Instead of going straight back to café, however, she took a walk around the park, exploring areas she had not yet visited. While it had initially felt like a big oval, she found that it was far larger than she had at first imagined. And while the area to the north was fenced off to contain the supposed bears and wolves she hadn't actually seen, to the east it was open, the rides and shops giving way to an open nature area. She came across a river flowing around the southern edge of the park, with a nature trail leading out into the forest.

She hadn't intended to follow it the whole way, but she soon found herself striding purposely down the trail. Virgin forest trees rose all around her, the vegetation thick and lush, something she had never seen on any Lake District documentaries. Jason had claimed it was left off most maps, and she could understand why. It was a magical place even without its connection to Christmas Land, a place where she could be at home with nature. She hummed quietly to herself as birds called from the trees, the leaves rustled overhead, and her feet made a soft crunch over the humus covering the trail.

After a couple of miles the trees began to thin out, the trail rising. She found the river again, winding its way through the forest, cascading white water stalling in wide, clear pools where fish darted in the shallows.

Open fell land began to replace forest, the ground continuing to rise. And then finally the forest was gone, and Bonnie stood by the edge of a pretty tarn, perhaps a hundred metres across. Fells rose around its sides, closing it again at the far side where a larger river sourced it, holding it like the cupping hands of a giant.

Birds called out of the water. A fish jumped. A huddle of ducks moved near the southern edge, upending into the water, searching for food, their contented quacks echoing back from the fells.

Bonnie breathed. Tears sprang to her eyes at the beauty of it all. She felt certain that if she climbed the fells on either side, she would find the Lake District spreading out around her, but here, in this hollow, she was perfectly alone.

A little bird watcher's hut stood among an area of reeds, reached by a wooden boardwalk. Bonnie walked across to it, stepping carefully over rotted planks. The hut, while not in disrepair, was shabby, a sign erected to identify various types of plant and animal life faded to illegibility. She was still on Christmas Land's property, and like everything else in the park, there was a sense of decay here, of neglect and abandonment. Out by the tarn, however, it felt okay, as though human interaction was unwanted, unnecessary.

Another path led around the shoreline, with others leading up to the ridgelines. Bonnie wasn't ready for such exertion, so she kept to the tarnside path, enjoying the sound of the ducks, the sight of a heron standing among reeds, some rabbits running among the grass on the lower slopes. On the other side of the tarn, a hiker's path was interrupted by an old sign that said PRIVATE PROPERTY, with a wooden fence keeping casual walkers away. She wondered again who owned it, who Mark had referred to as "the Boss". She would love a chance to meet them, particularly if….

'You're crazy to even think it,' she said aloud, entertained by the echo of her words across the fells. Even as she spoke, though, she felt what perhaps Mervin had, that this place was a special place within a larger special place, and it needed to be protected. Christmas Land, once in tune with the nature among which it lay, had lost its direction somewhere along the line.

There had to be something that could be done to restore the park while ensuring its impact on such a special environment was managed, to make sure that these forests and lakes were enjoyed yet protected. The world had become open and cruel, losing its magic. Somewhere like Christmas Land and its delicate environmental surrounds had the ability to give it back.

And from there, the goodwill could spread outwards—

Bonnie tripped on a loose root, losing her train of thought. 'Oh, dear,' she muttered, shaking her head, aware that she had been daydreaming, imagining the kind of things her father had talked about while putting her to bed. Somehow, over the last couple of days, she had become a child again, filled with a sense of wonder.

The walk back was a lot quicker, with the trail leading downhill most of the way. By the time she got back to the park, darkness had fallen and lights had come on, illuminating the walkways through the trees. It was still only four o'clock, though, so Bonnie bypassed the café and headed for the main entrance.

She found Brendon, dressed as Mr. Glockenspiel, sitting inside his gatehouse tower, reading a copy of *The Guardian*, one puffy trousered leg hooked over the other, a portable electric heater beside him to ward off the cold.

'Busy day?'

Brendon sat up. 'We've got two more guests due today,' he said. 'The last train stops at Ings Forest at four forty-five, so I'll be here another hour at least. How was your day?'

Bonnie smiled. 'Wonderful,' she said. 'Jason took us on a sleigh ride in the morning through the nature reserve. And I just got back from a walk up to the lake, I'm starving though. Lunch was a glass of sherry.'

Brendon smiled. 'It's easy to forget time here, isn't it? When the place begins to enchant you, you get drawn in. I can see from your eyes that you're on the way there. Are you still planning to leave?'

'I wanted to talk to you about that.'

'Sure.'

'I have to say, the idea is … tempting.'

Brendon smiled. 'Of course it is.'

'The problem is, I have a lot to lose. I can't just drop everything and move up here when it looks like the place is going to fall apart. I need some … guarantees.'

Even as she spoke she felt awkward, as though she were lost in a world where she didn't belong.

'There are no guarantees, I'm afraid,' Brendon said. 'However, it might be worth talking to someone who knew your uncle. I think you might then understand a little about what Christmas Land meant to him.'

Bonnie nodded. 'Sure,' she said. 'Who did you have in mind?'

'Well, the man's a bit of a legend, in the same way your

uncle was.' Brendon grimaced. 'He can come across a little … sharp. However, when you get to know him, you'll realise he's a big teddy bear.'

'Who?'

'His name's Gene Wilkins. He lives right on the edge of the park. If you can wait until the end of my shift, I'll take you over to visit him. Just … don't be scared, okay?'

16

GENE

AFTER THE TWO GUESTS, AN ELDERLY MALE COUPLE called John and Tim had arrived—collected from Ings Forest station by Jason and the sleigh—and settled into their chalet, Brendon led Bonnie across the park.

Past an area of pretty Christmas sculptures Brendon insisted looked best in the spring when they were adorned with flowers, he took them through a gate with a CLOSED sign hanging overhead, covering over the sign beneath.

Down a cobble path into a quiet glade, they approached a quaint log cabin. Eaves dappled with moss overhung a porch with a rocking chair outside. To the left of the cabin was another log building, with a tall, pointed roof and double doors that could open wide. A sign over the top read, FATHER CHRISTMAS'S COTTAGE.

'Gene is our resident big man during the main season,' Brendon explained. 'However, he's getting a little long in the tooth, so from this winter season his son, Ben, is set to take over. Gene's none too pleased, though. He wants to sit alongside and be known as "Grandfather Christmas" instead.'

'He sounds like a character.'

'Just you wait.'

Brendon, still dressed in costume, climbed up the step and knocked on the door. 'Um, Gene? Are you in there?'

Nothing happened. After a few seconds, Brendon lifted his hand to knock again, just as a side window swung open and a huge, grizzled, bearded face appeared.

'Get off my land!' the man bellowed.

Bonnie took a step back. On the step above, Brendon looked pained.

'Don't you know what season it is?' the man roared, shaking the window, and as if the shake was being passed along from one part of the house to the next, the entire porch began to tremble. Small trapdoors just big enough to put one's arm inside sprung upwards, and tendrils of smoke rose out. Then, to Bonnie's horror, green-clad arms appeared, hands reaching forward, claws glistening.

'I will not be disturbed until Christmas!' bellowed the man, and this time puffs of smoke came from overhead. More trapdoors opened in the underside of the eaves, this time plastic vines dropping down, dancing about like dangling snakes. Bonnie gasped with excitement, as Brendon gave her a pained look and then lifted his hands.

'Father, it is I, Mr. Glockenspiel, whom has awakened thee from your slumber. Please grant me an exception this time, and show yourself to your guests.'

With another growl that sounded pre-recorded, the face pulled back inside and the window slammed shut. An orchestrated reverberation shook the entire front of the house, making Bonnie jump. Then, with another puff of smoke, the front door swung open, revealing a towering, bearded man wearing only grey underwear and thick, knitted bed socks interwoven with reindeer and snowflake designs.

'Who has awoken me on this cool November day?' bellowed the man. 'Can't you wait until Christmas? Have you no patience? Will a present send you on your way?'

Brendon glanced back at Bonnie. 'Just say yes,' he hissed.

'Yes,' Bonnie said.

'Yes, what, child?'

'Yes, please.'

The towering figure relaxed. 'Then come into my house and choose.'

He stepped back. The smoke cleared, allowing Bonnie to see inside. The house was a treasure trove of children's toys, all lined up on shelves that reached to the ceiling. Dolls and soft toys filled one area, trucks and cars and toy soldiers for boys another.

'Do you have anything for adults?' Bonnie ventured.

The figure bowed, and lifted a hand to indicate a shelf laden with packaged cookies and fudge. Bonnie picked up a packet of toffees and smiled.

'Thank you very much, Father Christmas. It was lovely to meet you.'

'And you too, young lady.' He made another extravagant bow. Enjoy your visit to Christmas Land.'

A hand waved them towards the door. Brendon, however, stood his ground, lifting a hand.

'Um, Gene? That was magnificent as always. This is, um, Bonnie. Mervin's niece.'

Gene, still holding his position, looked up. 'Bonnie? Well, I never.'

'Thank you for your present,' she said, holding up the toffees. 'That was the first time I've ever met Father Christmas out of season, and it was, um, an experience.'

'The kids love it,' Brendon said. 'The park needed some way to incorporate a Father Christmas visit for the eleven months of the year when he's not in full Christmas mode. We sometimes have him out sweeping the paths, or pruning the bushes, always ready for a photograph, but a visit to his actual house is the most popular attraction. Everyone under sixteen gets a coupon for a prize, but they have to brave Father Christmas's grumpy porch first.'

Gene shrugged and gave an ambiguous grunt. Now that Bonnie got a good look at him, she could tell the beard was real, and the man hidden inside it was in his seventies at least, possibly older. He had a weariness to him which actually gave the character more life than she could have imagined. She wondered what he looked like in full Christmas regalia.

'Bonnie,' Gene said again. 'I can see Mervin in you. Come into my living room and share a cup of tea. Mr. Glockenspiel? Can you spare a moment too? It's been a while since I've had you over.'

Brendon winced at the use of his stage name and shook his head. 'I have to go and shut the main gates,' he said.

'Very well. I will entertain this young lady.'

As Brendon left, Gene led Bonnie through a door into a cozy, log cabin living room. To her surprise, a TV stood in one corner, but otherwise it was as rustic as a mountain lodge with an open fireplace, shelves of hardback books, a mantelpiece sparsely decorated with objects Gene had probably found in the forest. He waved Bonnie to an armchair, then disappeared through another door. She was still admiring the decoration when he reappeared a couple of minutes later and set a tray of tea and biscuits down on a coffee table. Then, with an enormous sigh, he slumped down into another armchair.

'Help yourself,' he said. 'I'm so pleased to see you. Any relative of Mervin's is a friend of mine.'

'Thank you.'

As she poured milk from a pretty floral jug into her tea, she told him about the lawyer's letter, and how she had come with her friend to take a look at what Mervin had left her. Gene nodded along, muttering under his breath, his eyes closed as though he had drifted off into a fitful sleep.

'And Mr. Glockenspiel—or whatever his name is—brought you to me in order to convince you to stay?' he said when she was finished, his eyes still closed.

Bonnie nodded. 'Something like that. You see, I can really feel the pull of this place, but I won't just drop everything and move up here. It's too much. I'm not rich, or full of energy anymore. I don't know how to run a café, and I can't cook—'

Gene lifted a hand. 'There are a lot of don'ts, can'ts, aren'ts and won'ts in what you say,' he said, his eyes still closed. 'How about you rephrase a few things?'

'Like, how?'

'Cooking can be learned. Running a café can be learned. Age is a state of mind. Your uncle, he loved this place. His café remained a centerpiece of Christmas Land until his death. Everyone who came here went away with a little touch of magic in their hearts. Even when the numbers fell, when the park began to fall into disrepair, he never gave up. I talked to him the day before he died, and he assured me that he had everything in hand, that this year's Christmas would be the greatest of them all, and Christmas Land would rise once again.'

'And the next day he was dead?'

'Of a heart attack. He was an old man.'

'I thought you said age was a state of mind?'

Gene's huge beard shifted, and Bonnie sensed a smile hidden beneath. 'It is until it catches up with you. Believe me, until the day he died, Mervin felt as young as the day he arrived. We had a good life here, me and him, and the others.'

The lively, jubilant character Bonnie had first encountered was gone. Gene seemed to shrink in the chair, a shadow of the man he had been.

'What's going to happen to the park if it continues to decline?'

Gene sighed. 'I received a letter last spring,' he said. 'Mervin received the same letter. It was sent to all senior members of the park. It talked about the end, about how the park was no longer sustainable, how it would need to be closed if we couldn't do something about it. This is a wonderland, for sure, but it's also a business. And a business that has no customers ceases to operate.'

'That makes sense, I suppose.'

'Mervin had a plan,' he said. 'The park would recover, become popular again, rise from the ashes. People had stopped believing, he told me. Modern life with all its ease and its negativity had flushed out the last of the magic. Everything had become political, everything had become offensive. We had to go back to basics, he told me, but we also had to embrace the future. You see, while I'm merely an actor, Mervin was a businessman. Then he died, taking his plans with him, and leaving us to face the inevitable end.'

Bonnie sighed. 'It doesn't sound like there's much hope.'

'Oh, there's plenty of that. But sometimes, whether we like it or not, hope isn't all that's necessary. We need knowledge.'

17

LOVE RITES

Bonnie was lost in thought as she headed back to the café. Starving, she had polished off most of the toffees by the time she got there. She went upstairs, made herself a sandwich, and then went back down, turned on the café lights and sat at a table by the window, looking out at the plaza's glittery splendour. It seemed so sad that such a place would have to close, particularly when it clearly meant so much for so many people. There was no denying the passage of time, though, and no matter what Uncle Mervin had planned, it might not have been enough.

Now that she was back, though, she wondered just what his plan had been. Perhaps there was some clue in his secret room upstairs.

Debbie was still out, so Bonnie went up through the hidden door to Mervin's grotto. She stared at his cluttered desk, feeling uncomfortable about going through his personal papers so soon, so instead turned to his bookshelves, trying to get an understanding of the man her uncle had once been.

His love for Christmas was immediately apparent. His

collection of books on the subject bordered on scholarly, but Bonnie found everything from crinkly histories of Medieval traditions to books on Christmas decoration paper crafts, speculative symbolism theory to colourfully decorated children's poems. While some books were almost new, others were so old they were possibly of great value. Bonnie had a flick through the pages of some, but found the language tough to understand.

Then there were wider-branching books on religious symbolism and festivals around the world, suggesting that Mervin had been something of an authority on the way people liked to enjoy themselves. Bonnie took out a large picture book on world festivals and spent a few minutes flicking through colourful pictures of celebrations such as South Korea's Boryeong Mud Festival to La Tomatina in Spain.

On one corner shelf she found a couple of dozen cooking books, mostly based on drinks and snacks. One was entitled *101 Ways to Enjoy Hot Chocolate*, while another was *Snacks and Cakes from the Ancient World*. Bonnie took both down, using the indexes to find the relevant sections on marshmallows. It was true, then, that original marshmallows had been made using the mallow plant, *althea officianalis*, which had grown in marshes in ancient Egypt. She was surprised to find that there were several hundred other recipes, none of which included the gelatin she had always assumed was necessary. She shook her head as she turned the pages and looked at the glossy pictures of marshmallows in all shapes, colours, and sizes.

It was making her feel hungry. Her coffee cup was empty too, so she carried the two books downstairs and set about rooting through the cupboards to see if Mervin had left any ingredients behind. She was just brewing up another pot of coffee when she heard someone stumping up the stairs.

Debbie slouched into the room and dropped down on the sofa. 'Battered,' she said, glancing up at Bonnie. 'This place rocks.'

'Good night?'

Debbie shook her head and let out a long sigh. 'We're in the pub when the door opens and Father Christmas walks in. Oh, man. It was epic. He was in full Victorian gear, all green woodsman set up. Massive beard. Just huge. Has a Christmas tree over his shoulder, just like in the pictures on them old Christmas cards. And he buys us all a pint. Just … incredible.'

Debbie was clearly drunk. Bonnie handed her a coffee just as Debbie started to cry. Bonnie lifted an eyebrow, unsure what to say.

'And then he whips out this pack of cards and starts pulling off all these card tricks. Like, proper badass stuff. Couldn't pick any of it. Me and the lads, we're just like … mind blown.'

'You got drunk with Father Christmas?'

'Only like one pint. He said he had to get back to work and headed out. Yeah, I know it was a dude in a suit, whatever. But he looked so *real*.'

'Sounds great.'

Debbie started crying again. 'This is the best holiday ever,' she said. 'I don't want it to end.'

'Well, we can probably hang on a couple more days before the Old Ragtag sees through my lie and either fires me or hunts me down.'

'I want to stay forever.'

'Really? Perhaps you can manage the café.'

Debbie looked up, eyes going wide. Her black eyeliner had run, giving her huge panda eyes. She looked like an extra from a zombie movie. Bonnie couldn't help but laugh.

'Are you serious?' Debbie said. 'I could totally do it. I mean, we'd have to paint the windows black and get some posters up, but it could totally be done.'

'I've been thinking about it,' Bonnie said. She held up the two books she had brought down from the grotto upstairs. 'I was doing some background reading, I guess you'd call it. I've never been much of a cook, and Phil used to run me down about it all the time, so after he left, I got lazy. Pasta was about my limit. It can't be that hard to make something simple, though, can it? I mean, the instructions are all here.'

'Ancient recipes?' Debbie said. 'Awesome.'

'You reckon you can get out of bed tomorrow morning to help me?'

'Hell yeah. I'm meeting Mitchell and the lads for lunch, but before that—'

Debbie suddenly broke down in another flood of tears. Bonnie couldn't remember her crying so much since they had forced themselves to sit through the heartbreaking end of *Hachi*. Neither had cried over Richard Gere's death, but the old dog limping to the train station … they'd had to pause it while they commandeered a toilet roll from the bathroom.

'What is it?' Bonnie asked.

'It's Mitchell,' Debbie said. 'They're going home tomorrow. I might never see them again.'

'Did something happen between you?'

Debbie flapped her hands. 'Sort of, yeah. He held my hand and said he liked my sense of fashion. Did you know he used to drum in a metal band?'

'I'm more surprised that it appears he can speak.'

Debbie shook her head. 'Not at all,' she said. 'He's deaf.'

'Really?'

'He said he had an accident when he was eighteen. Lost his hearing. Had to give up the band, although he said he still drums sometimes. Likes to feel the beat in his hands.'

Bonnie felt insensitive about asking, but she really wanted to know and knew Debbie would tell her while she was drunk. 'But if he's deaf, surely he can still speak?'

'He said it's been a while, and he's kind of forgotten. He was always pretty quiet, he said, but since losing his hearing he's lost much of the will to speak. Personally, I think he just likes to appear mysterious.'

'For a self-professed quiet guy, he seems to have a lot to say. Did he tell you all this?'

Debbie shook her head. 'He wrote it on his phone. Says he's going to teach me to sign, too. He's still learning.'

'Oh.' Bonnie smiled. 'But that's good, isn't it? If he's talking about you in a future sense it means he wants to see you after you leave here. Didn't you say they were from Bristol? That's only a fifteen minute train ride.'

'It won't be the same!' Debbie wailed. 'The magic is here. You can't top a Christmas romance. You can't just go back to real life. It's not the same.'

Bonnie remembered what Gene had said. Uncle Mervin had believed people took a little of the magic of Christmas Land home with them. Even among the overgrown ruins of the neglected park, there was enough magic left that Debbie could feel it. It was still there, simmering under the surface, waiting for its chance to step back into the sunlight.

'Tomorrow we make marshmallows,' she said, clapping Debbie on the shoulder. 'Are you in?'

Debbie's lip trembled, but for now she held the tears inside. 'You're going to save the park, aren't you?'

'I wouldn't go that far.'

'You can do it,' Debbie said. 'Then Mitchell and me can be together forever.' And with that, she burst into a fresh flood of tears.

18

MARSHMALLOW MARSHES

As always, Debbie looked bright and breezy the next morning. Bonnie, on the other hand, had a coffee hangover from a restless night and felt stiff after a second night in a strange bed. Rather than eat breakfast at home, they headed straight out to the Mountain Breeze, where Debbie ordered a repeat of the monstrosity from the morning before. Bonnie, with nothing like her friend's appetite, ordered a simple slice of toast, although when it arrived, jam had been spread across it in a shape that resembled a robin sitting on a branch.

They weren't the only customers this morning. The elderly male couple, John and Tim, sat a couple of tables across, peering at a map.

'Aren't they cute?' Debbie whispered.

Bonnie had never considered old men to be cute, but Debbie had a point. From the way the pair smiled and laughed at each other, it was clear they were far more than friends. For a moment she had a brief pang of loneliness, but she shook it off. The last few years of her marriage to Phil had been cagey and full of lies and secrets. She knew exactly what he was doing, but could never call him on it for risking a huge blowout in front of her children, both going through difficult teenage years at the time. Now that she looked back on it, a lot of pain and hassle could have been saved, but hindsight was a beautiful thing. At the time it had just been easier to go through the motions, ignoring their problems like a child refusing to wave his father off to sea. By the time she looked up and took notice, the ship was too far out.

The two old men had finished their breakfast. They stopped next to Bonnie and Debbie's table as they headed for the door, one of them tipping the edge of the floppy hat he wore.

'Good morning, ladies,' he said. 'Isn't it a lovely day? Are you both staying here, too?'

'Just for a few days,' Bonnie said.

'Actually, she owns Mervin's Marshmallow Café,' Debbie said, throwing Bonnie a sideways look that said, *you're not leaving if I can help it.* 'It's just under refurbishment.'

'Oh, what a shame,' the elderly gentleman said. 'We would love to stop by for a drink sometime. John here can't eat sugar because of his diabetes, but I love a marshmallow or two.'

'Or three,' John said. 'Ted eats them for me.'

The two old men seemed happy to chat, so Bonnie asked them how they had come by the park.

'Every year we spent our Christmases at a little place in Scotland,' John said. 'Christmas means so much to both of us, for one reason or another. Unfortunately, the village we always visit is closed until December, so we were hunting around online for something else to do—we don't like to sit still at our age, don't you know? We might not have much longer—and we came across this park.

The advert was a little dated, but we're still glad we came.'

'I was expecting more places to be open,' Ted said, but it's nice that its quiet, and we love the nature. We might look on our last legs, but we're not dead yet. We're heading up to the lake this morning. We're both keen birdwatchers, and there's nothing quite like watching birds over a flask of hot chocolate and a mince pie.'

They wished Debbie and Bonnie a good day and then headed out. Debbie turned to Bonnie, grinning. 'Oh, they're so cute,' she said. 'Look at them. They must be at least a hundred years old, but they're so in love, you can just tell. God, I wish my life didn't suck and I could find someone to love me like that.'

'What about Mitchell?'

Debbie rolled her eyes. 'Come on,' she said. 'I've only known him a couple of days. Think I'd give up my chastity so easily?'

'That's not what you were saying last night.'

Debbie rolled her eyes again. 'What happens on the beer, stays on the beer. Are we going to go wade through muck and dig up plants or what?'

Bonnie smiled. 'Let's go.'

∾

Out past Ings Forest station, a series of boardwalks had been set up to allow people to walk among the marshland boarding the lake without getting their feet wet. The river that flowed through Christmas Land exited here in this lake, which they learned from a sign was called Grunnerfell Water. The same sign said that "Grunnr" was an old Norse word that meant "shallow", and that the lake was no more than two metres at its deepest point, most of it much shallower. And except during heavy rain, much of it was semi-waterlogged marsh. Finding a bench overlooking an area thick with flowers and plants, Bonnie pulled out her recipe book and found a picture of the flower they were looking for. It wasn't hard to find; the mallow plant grew everywhere here.

'Are we allowed to just pick it?' Debbie said. 'Won't we get fined or something?'

'I'm not sure about that,' Bonnie said. 'I heard from Brendon that Uncle Mervin picked his plants here, but it seems like he was a bit of a conservationist, so perhaps he has a special place somewhere. Best just get a couple to be safe. I only want to do a quick experiment.'

The nearest mallow plants were a few feet away from the boardwalk. Neither had thought to bring any boots, so they played rock-scissors-paper to decide who would wade out into the water. Bonnie guessed correctly that Debbie would subconsciously choose rock, and then used the same tactic to win both the best of three, best of five, and finally the best of seven before Debbie reluctantly began to unlace her boots, grumbling about sharks and crabs.

'You're much younger than me,' Bonnie said. 'The cold will probably give me a heart attack. Remember, we need a chunk of the root. Since we're likely to go to environmental hell for this, try not to pull up the whole plant. Just break a bit off.'

'Cool name for a band, that.'

'What?'

'Environmental hell.'

'Maybe there's a Christmas concert you could perform at.'

'Providing I don't drown.'

With a great deal of fanfare, Debbie climbed down into the marshy water, sods of springy grass contracting to soak her almost to her knees. Grumbling with each step, she reached the nearest mallow plant, rolled up her sleeves, and plunged her arms into the muck.

'Oh, god, this is rank. I can feel something biting me.'

'Could be a snake,' Bonnie said, trying to look serious. 'Quick, grab the root before it realises you're potential food.'

Debbie, scowling, felt around in the water, then stood up with something mucky and stringy in her hands. When Bonnie nodded, she retreated with the speed of a pirate who has just recovered treasure in crocodile-infested waters, scrambling back to the boardwalk and hauling herself out.

'I know you probably thought you were having a laugh, but I totally felt something down there,' she muttered, pulling off her jumper and using it to dry her feet. 'I'm sure I felt teeth. Do leeches have teeth?'

'No, but sea monsters do,' Bonnie said. 'A good job you got your arm out of there. The poor thing was nearly poisoned.' Then, picking up the lump of root Debbie had unceremoniously dumped on the boardwalk, she smiled and said, 'Good work, my dear. Now, let's go and cook.'

19

CULINARY ADVENTURES

'Right,' Bonnie said, pointing at the recipe book. 'First we have to make this lump of gunk into a powder.'

'How do we do that?'

'We have to chop it up really fine and sun-dry it.'

'It's November! There isn't any sun!'

'We'd better make one, then. You chop. I'll see what I can find.'

As Debbie got to work with the knife, dicing the piece of root, Bonnie hurried upstairs to see what she could find. Five minutes later she was back down with a desktop lamp and a hairdryer.

'Rustic,' Debbie muttered.

'It works for incubating chicks,' Bonnie said. 'Chop it a bit finer, then put it on this bread board.'

'Why the bread board?'

'Wood will hold the heat. Then, if we make a little wall with this foil, it'll keep the heat in.'

'Looks good. What about the hairdryer?'

'We'll give it a blast to get rid of some of the moisture.'

'Make sure to keep it on a low setting though, so it doesn't blast bits everywhere.'

'Good point.'

As she set Debbie to work again, she wandered around the café until she found what she was looking for: a wall radiator on which she could balance the breadboard, with a plug socket nearby for the lamp.

'Right, bring it over here and we're all set up.'

'Won't we burn the café down putting it up there?'

Bonnie shook her head. 'Nope. Not with someone watching it just in case. That's your job.'

'What about you?'

'I need to find an egg. We need egg whites for this.'

'Egg?'

'Kind of oval, comes from a chicken. There were some in Uncle Mervin's fridge … but they'd kind of evolved into higher life-forms.'

Debbie wrinkled her nose. 'Brutal.'

'Just sit here and read a magazine or something. I'll nip over to the café.'

She left Debbie with the drying power and jogged across the plaza to the Mountain Breeze. June was on duty, standing behind the counter reading a horse-riding magazine. Christmas songs tinkled in the background, and a coffee machine hummed in the corner.

'Can I borrow an egg?' Bonnie asked. 'Just one will be enough … for now.'

'I can cook you one up if you're hungry,' June said, putting her magazine down. 'I haven't had a customer since this morning.'

Bonnie shook her head. 'I'm doing some baking,' she said.

'Oh?'

Bonnie grinned. 'Marshmallows.'

'Right. Got it. Wait here.'

June darted into the backroom, returning with an egg box. 'Take them all,' she said. 'We've got the supplier coming in the morning.'

'The supplier?'

'They come up a forest road into the back of the park. Only deliveries, no customers. Why … do you need something ordered?'

Bonnie lifted a hand. 'Not quite yet, but we'll see.'

'Sounds very exciting.'

'Maybe.'

Bonnie thanked June for the eggs and hurried back across the plaza. Halfway across, she spotted the two old gentlemen they had met in the Mountain Breeze earlier, sitting on a bench near the central fountain.

'Good afternoon,' one of them called, the other lifting an arm to wave. 'We couldn't help but notice the lights were on in the café. Are you open? It had such great reviews online.'

Bonnie grimaced. 'Possibly. If you can wait an hour. I'm baking.' She glanced down at her watch. 'Come back at three o'clock. I can't guarantee there'll be anything worth eating or drinking, but you never know. I'm not the best of cooks, but, well, I—'

Her voice had taken on a high-pitched note. She decided to shut up before she said something ridiculous.

'Three o'clock it is,' John said.

'We're looking forward to it,' said Ted.

Bonnie hurried into the café. 'How are we doing?'

Debbie had found a science fiction novel from somewhere and was sitting with her feet up on one of the tables, the book in one hand, the hairdryer on a low setting in the other.

'We're rocking it,' she said. 'Totally almost there.'

'Good. Let me have a look.'

What had formerly been a lumpy piece of root now resembled flour. Bonnie smiled. 'Let's grind it a little more, then have a go at cooking with it. I got eggs.'

'Nice. What are they for?'

'Making the marshmallow fluffy.'

Debbie took her feet off the table and sat up. 'You're all flustered,' she said. 'Look at you, anyone would think you'd been doing exercise or something. You're loving this, aren't you?'

Bonnie couldn't keep the smile off her face. She shifted from foot to foot like a toddler wanting to pee. 'Makes you feel alive, doesn't it?'

'Cooking?'

Bonnie shrugged. She had been thinking more along the lines of breaking out of a comfort zone, but cooking worked pretty well too.

'You break the eggs, I'll whisk,' she said.

'Do we have a whisk?'

Bonnie shook her head. 'I have no idea.'

∽

After Mervin's death, the café had been closed down, everything put away and disposable food stuffs thrown out, but in the cupboards Bonnie found all manner of cooking utensils and appliances. She came across a huge industrial whisk, but the sheer size of the thing was overwhelming. Instead, she emerged from the kitchen with a wire hand whisk, brandishing it like a weapon.

Once the egg was fluffy, she ground the drying powder some more, then mixed a little of it with water until it became a thick paste. She had been unable to find corn syrup so poured a jar of maple syrup into a pan, then took a plastic tub with SUGAR written in pen on the lid and poured some in. After it had heated to 121C, the optimum, according to the recipe, for marshmallows, she mixed it with the egg and started whisking again.

'You want to swap?' Debbie said after a couple of minutes. Bonnie, sweating as her right arm threatened to seize up, nodded. 'We'll take it in turns,' she gasped.

By the time the mixture was sufficiently thick enough to pour onto a tray and allow to set, Bonnie was eying the industrial whisk with frustration. Preparing enough homemade marshmallows to feed a café full of people, it made perfect sense.

'Right, we're good,' she said, sprinkling the thick, white paste with icing sugar. 'We'll let it set for a while. Go and find the lads. You can call in those two old chaps from the square, too. I'll make some tea. We might as well make a party of it.'

'Are you sure?'

Bonnie wasn't sure she could speak without breaking into that creepy high-pitched titter that always came when she was excited. Instead she just smiled and shrugged.

'All right,' Debbie said. 'Back in a bit.'

Bonnie loaded the marshmallows into a big industrial fridge in the café's kitchen. Unable to concentrate on anything else while they cooled, she hopped nervously from foot to foot, occasionally opening the fridge to peer inside as though expecting some dramatic transformation.

Finally, with an hour passed, she withdrew the tray and set it down on a countertop. The mixture looked pretty unimpressive, but when she prodded it with a fork, it squished appreciatively like a sponge, bringing a smile to Bonnie's face. Through the door out of the kitchen into the café, she heard the main door open, Debbie returning with the group of first tasters. With her heart pounding,

Bonnie scooped up the tray and carried it through into the café.

Debbie had already arranged the crowd onto a long wooden bench. Larry, Barry and Mitchell sat alongside John and Ted. June had come across from the Mountain Breeze, bringing Niall with her. Sitting on the end were Shaun from the elf crew and Jason, the reindeer handler.

'We got enough to go round?' Debbie asked.

Bonnie nodded as she took a knife and cut the mixture into squares before scooping the marshmallows out on to a serving platter. 'Plenty. No one eat until I say the word.'

'I'll pass,' John said, as the others took a marshmallow off the tray. He patted his chest. 'Diabetes. It's a real mood hoover.'

'We've got a lovely salad in the fridge at the chalet,' Ted said, grinning. 'Best that we don't both spoil our appetites. I'll suffer for both of us.'

'They're a bit wonky,' Larry said, turning his over. 'Not like the ones you get in the shop.'

'These are ten times better,' Bonnie said, before adding, 'I hope.' She glanced around the group. 'Ready? On three. One, two … three.'

Everyone stuffed their marshmallows into their mouths. Bonnie realised that in the excitement she had forgotten to take one for herself, but figured she'd be biased anyway, as the cook. Best to see their reactions first.

Mitchell and Barry grimaced. Larry spat his out. Shaun let out a whimper of pain as he swallowed and then scratched the scar beside his nose. Jason and Niall forcibly swallowed theirs, then glanced at each other as though conspirators in some heist. June, who had only taken a small bite, stared at the remainder as though the grey-brown blob better belonged in the bin.

'Lovely,' Barry muttered.

June forced a smile. Jason stared at his hands.

Bonnie felt the colour draining out of her face. After all that effort she had failed. The wave of elation she had felt as she handed out the marshmallows fell away, and she reached for the back of a chair as her knees began to tremble.

'I'm sorry,' she began, but Debbie put up a hand.

'I think I see the problem.' No one looked up, so Debbie turned to Bonnie, a wide grin on her face. 'What a pair of muppets we are,' she said, nodding at the countertop where they had lined up the plastic containers they had found in the kitchen cupboard. 'I think someone put the lids on wrong.' She pulled off the lid labeled SALT, dipped a finger in, and, much to the horror of those assembled, poked the white-powdered digit into her mouth. 'Yep. That'll be it. I've found the sugar.'

As though someone had broken a spell, the group around the table burst into laughter. Bonnie felt tears spring to her eyes but she was laughing with them at the inanity of their oversight. Glancing behind her at the mixture they had left to cook, she said, 'Would it be possible for you to all come back again in half an hour? I think we need to make a couple of minor adjustments to the mix.'

Larry and Barry clapped. June wiped a tear out of her eye. The others were grinning. John leaned across the table and picked up one of the remaining marshmallows on the tray.

'No sugar?' he said. 'In that case, I might as well indulge.'

20

DOWN TO BUSINESS

By nine-pm, the café was full. Half of the park's staff had shown up for the impromptu party, as well as most of the currently guests, including a couple of families with young children who now played in the children's play area at the back. Long out of marshmallow mix, instead the café owners on the staff had donated boxes of biscuits and cookies. The lads had brought in some craft beers from the pub and now sat on one table, playing team Jenga against the three elves who sat opposite, fully decked out in their staff gear. Jason, who had gone home to change clothes, had reappeared just after dark by sleigh, bringing with him a couple of boxes of Christmas lights, which they had all helped to hang up over the café's front windows while the four reindeer snorted and stamped outside the front door.

Debbie, holding a can of Guinness, leaned on Bonnie's shoulder.

'We're close,' she said. 'That fourth batch was nearly spot on. Did you see Mitchell's eyes when he popped that marshmallow into his mouth? Sometimes it doesn't take words, Bon.'

'We'll go up and get some more root in the morning,' Bonnie said. 'June told me that if we walk around the lake a little way, we'll come to a fenced section which belonged to Mervin. She said it's probably in the deeds to the café somewhere.'

'Tomorrow,' Debbie said. 'I don't want to think about tomorrow.'

'It could be the start of the rest of our lives.'

'Or the end.'

Bonnie sighed. 'I told you, they only live in Bristol. If you had a job, you'd probably commute there to work every day.'

'I could never work with a broken heart.'

'Well, it's not broken yet. And if it is, we could probably fix it with a few spoonfuls of marshmallow mix.'

'Are you making fun of me?'

Before Bonnie could answer, the Jenga tower crashed down with the clatter of wooden bricks. A cheer rose from the elves as Larry thumped the tabletop and yelled, 'Best of seven!' at the top of his voice.

'I'll miss this place,' Debbie said. 'It won't be the same when the lads are gone, though.'

'Other people will come.'

'Will they?'

'Sure. If they know it's here.'

Debbie lifted her head to look into Bonnie's eyes. 'And will you be here?'

'I might be. Depends.'

'You're going to stay, aren't you?'

Bonnie sighed. 'I still don't know. It's a big ask. I need to do so much before I can even think about it. But … I am thinking about it. This place, it's special. It's what I've dreamed of my whole life. Everything that I ever had and worked hard for, it got taken away. My marriage, my family, my hopes of ever getting a decent job … in the end I lost it all and I ended up with nothing. You don't understand because you're still young. You can still dream that things will get better. I was just treading water, trying to keep my head up, trying to stay afloat … I had no more dreams.' She shrugged. 'And then this came out of nowhere. I feel like I've been given a second chance. My mind is fighting so hard to make me give it up, to walk away, to go back to my crappy Morrico job and my pokey little house on my grey, boring street … but my heart, it wants me to stay. And I'm worried that if I go, it won't follow. It'll leave me behind.'

'Man, that's awesome,' Debbie said. 'You're like, totally being life-changed.'

'Thanks,' Bonnie said. 'I think.'

She was about to say something more when the front door opened. A gust of cold air whipped around their faces as a tall figure stepped inside.

'Ho ho ho!' hollered Gene, dressed in a splendid Victorian Father Christmas costume. 'Wouldn't be a Christmas party without the big man himself!'

He dropped a box down on the nearest table with the clink of wine bottles, then reached inside and pulled out a pack of cards.

'Who wants to see some magic?' he roared, as around Bonnie, the crowd cheered.

~

It felt strange to be back in Quimbeck after three days in the forests of Christmas Land, but Bonnie needed supplies. She still hadn't made up her mind what to do, but it didn't hurt to be prepared. Down a side street, she found a small supermarket, so she stocked up on foodstuffs she would need to make a few more batches of marshmallows. In a stockroom at the back of the café she had come across a box of old menus, so picked up a few random ingredients in order to add a little variation to the basic mix. It seemed Uncle Mervin had been an experimenter, always trying new recipes for marshmallows, adding them to a variety of hot chocolate mixes of his own design, and now that the shock of her first effort was a distant memory, Bonnie found it exciting to try new ideas. It was liberating, as though she was casting off the shackles of her old life one marshmallow at a time.

While in Quim, she called work, her hand shaking as the Old Ragtag came on the line.

'Are you feeling better?' he asked. 'Or are you milking a little sniffle for everything it's worth?'

'I've never felt so sick,' Bonnie said, dramatically coughing into the phone and then holding a hand over the receiver while she laughed. Then, speaking as fast as she could, she said, 'The doctor said I have 'sickasaparrotitis.'

'I've not heard of that. Is it serious.'

'I'd infect half the staff if I came back,' she said. 'Best to stay away until it's cleared.'

'If you're not back by next Monday I'll start docking your holiday allotment,' the Old Ragtag said without a hint of sympathy.

'I'll try to shake it off by then,' Bonnie said, giving him another dramatic cough.

As she hung up, she couldn't keep the grin off her face. It had been Debbie's idea to prank her boss, and she felt so exhilarated by doing something she would never have dared to do before, that she stopped by The King's Thistle for a drink before heading back.

Len was surprised to see her. 'Looks like you've decided to stay around,' he said, glancing at her shopping bags. 'Things are going okay up there, are they?'

Bonnie smiled. 'It's a bit rough around the edges,' she said. 'But the deeper you delve, the more you find.'

'Good for you. Are you planning to stay for a while, then?'

'At least until the weekend. After that, I don't know. I'm thinking about it.'

'You must see more in that place than most of us do. It's a terrible eyesore.'

Bonnie shrugged. 'It has a certain charm if you know how to see it.' She thought about Brendon in his ridiculous costume, Gene and his refusal to drop character, Jason and his reindeer, the elves … it was rough around the edges, and it did feel like a calamitous ship about to sink, yet there was something there. Something worth throwing a lifebelt for, and pulling like damn hell on the rope to bring it back in.

'Do you like marshmallows?' she asked.

'Um, well, I suppose I don't mind the odd one.'

Bonnie picked up her glass of sherry and downed it in one swift gulp. Then, reaching down into her bag, she pulled out a paper bag of marshmallows leftover from the most recent batch.

'A present,' she said, handing them to Len.

'Well, don't mind if I do,' he said, plucking one out of the bag and popping it into his mouth. 'Wow, that's rather good.'

Bonnie smiled. 'If you want more, you'll have to come up to Mervin's Marshmallow Café in Christmas Land sometime. I've decided to reopen.'

'If they all taste like that, you'll get plenty of customers,' Len said.

Bonnie grinned. 'Thank you. And thanks for the drink. I'll stop by for another next time I'm in the village.'

'I'm already looking forward to it,' Len said.

~

'You look drunk,' Debbie said, looking up from the sofa as Bonnie came in.

Bonnie shook her head. 'Just drunk on life,' she said. 'You know, for once.'

'I wish I was drunk,' Debbie said. 'But I needed a shoulder to cry on.'

'Again?'

'The lads have gone back. Mitchell said he'll text me when he gets back to Bristol.'

'That's good, isn't it?'

'I don't know, is it?'

Bonnie shrugged. 'I'm a little out of the relationships loop, but it sounds promising.'

Debbie sighed. 'Maybe. What am I supposed to do now?'

'You could help me give this place a clean. It's a bit dusty. I don't think anyone has touched it since Uncle Mervin died.'

'You're going to reopen?'

Bonnie winced. Her head still held sway, controlling her heart's wishing. 'Maybe,' she said.

'You know, I said it before, but if you want, I'll stay here and help. I mean, I'll need time off to go to metal festivals and stuff, and I'd need to call Mum and let her know, since she thinks we've just gone on holiday, but … you know….'

'I'd love it if you wanted to help. But what about Mitchell?'

Debbie shrugged. 'I'm not sure it would work outside of Christmas Land. I don't know. I don't want to take the risk that if I saw him in Bristol he'd seem kind of … ordinary.'

'A deaf drummer could never be ordinary.'

'Yeah, but you know.'

'It won't have the same spark?'

'Something like that.'

'Plus, I was talking to that elf guy this morning….'

'What elf guy?'

'Shaun. The one with the scar by his nose. Did you know he had a bit part in *Doctor Sleep*?'

Bonnie shook her head. 'I didn't know that.'

'He was "man in car park number four" in the credits. He got paid eighty quid.'

'Wow.'

'That was like a massive horror movie.'

'Isn't he a bit old for you?'

'He's thirty-five. That's nothing.'

Bonnie smiled. 'How about we talk about it while we clean the café downstairs? Then we'll have another go at making marshmallows. I reckon I'm getting the hang of it.'

'Cool. Let's go. Say, if we open the café, do I have to wear some stupid Christmas jumper?'

'I guess it depends on the season.'

'Black's kind of a symbol of winter, isn't it?'

'I suppose so. If you got a bit of icing sugar on it, you could claim it was the night sky, couldn't you?'

21

THE TREE

When Bonnie woke up on Thursday morning, her arms and shoulders ached like they hadn't done in years. She had certainly never put in the same effort while mopping the floors at Morrico, but the result was that the café downstairs was now sparkling and clean. A couple of hours in, Jason the reindeer handler and June's son Niall had stopped by and offered to help. Together, they had set out all the remaining tables and chairs and tidied up the kitchen, making sure everything was in the correctly labeled box. Afterwards, Bonnie had treated her group of helpers to her latest attempt at hot chocolate.

The response had been positive.

Debbie had planned to go out early, taking a nature trail walk with Shaun, who had a day off. Her bed was empty, but for the first time neatly made. With a smile, Bonnie wondered if Christmas Land was having an effect on her rebellious best friend. Perhaps in the end she might start wearing colours, or at least brighter shades of black.

Bonnie decided to take a walk of her own before settling down to work. She had discovered a series of colour-coded trails crisscrossed the park, taking in themed attractions depending on your interest. She chose the Yellow Trail, which focused on Father Christmas and his toy factory, leading her across the park to Gene's house, then back along the northern side, past several themed toy shops, one focused on wooden products, another on European traditional toys. Both were closed, their windows grimy. From there, it led her down into a corner of the park, where she found a closed attraction called the Living Toyshop Maze. Peering through dirty windows, inside were rows of human-sized toy costumes lined up against a wall.

Finally the trail led her back around to the main entrance, and a visit with Mr. Glockenspiel. She found Brendon inside his gatehouse, this time reading a book.

'I need to talk with you,' she said. 'And not just you, but everyone who has a permanent stake in this place.'

'Why?'

'Because I need some guarantees. Not because it's particularly romantic or festive, but because I need to have a clearer idea of what's going on, and what's likely to happen.' She planted her hands on her hips. 'The truth is, I'm pulling a sickie from work to be here. If I'm not back by Monday, my boss is going to start asking serious questions, and knowing that old goat, I'll be unemployed by Friday. While the temptation to move up here and make a go of things is overwhelming, I'm too old to put my entire livelihood on the line if the park is going to shut in a couple of months. Merry Christmas, here's a cardboard box for you to live in.'

'I see.'

'I'm not getting any younger, and no one has my back. I'm divorced, and being unemployed won't pay the mortgage my ex-husband left me with. Do you see where I'm coming from?'

'I do.'

Bonnie sighed, aware she had begun to rant. She let the stillness of the park flood back in, the chirp of the birds in the trees, the rustle of the wind, the distant cry of a reindeer and the light background tinkle of Christmas music.

'Everyone talks about Christmas magic, but I grew out of that when my father died. I was forced to become practical, and adapt, and I can't just throw in my life for some whim, no matter how tempting.'

'Sure.'

'I need to know that I'm not going to waste my efforts, that I'm going to come out of this with something to show for it, or at the very least not be broke, unemployed, and homeless.'

'Right.'

Bonnie looked at Brendon, for the first time really seeing the costume that could have come from the set of a version of Alice in Wonderland. As if to emphasise the point, he shifted in his seat, the interactive musical instrument fitted into his back giving a little tinkle. Bonnie couldn't help but smile.

'So … what are we going to do about it?'

Brendon closed his newspaper. 'I can see this is something you've thought long and hard about,' he said. 'How about we have a meeting tonight at the Mountain Breeze? It's a little nicer than the staff centre. Then we can see where things are. I can put the word out this morning.'

'Please do.'

Brendon smiled. 'You just need to be convinced, then?'

'What?'

'I'm glad you'll be joining us.'

'I didn't say that.'

'You just did. You pretty much just told me to organise

a meeting to convince you to stay here in Christmas Land. All we need to do is say the right things, and you'll be one of us? June will be delighted. Most of the staff members are men, and she's always telling me she wants someone to talk to about women's stuff. I mean, there's Belinda who runs Lapland Costumes at the far end of the park, but she's pushing eighty.'

'I haven't said I'm going to stay. Look, there seems to be very little in the way of forward thinking going on here. Everyone is content to let life pass them by.'

'The park looks wonderful in snow. This valley gets on average four times the rest of the Lake District. It can pile right up, sometimes.'

'That's all well and good, but it won't matter if the park gets bulldozed, will it?'

Brendon smiled. 'Okay, I'll call the meeting. Shall we say, eight o'clock?'

'Perfect. I'll see you at the Mountain Breeze.'

She left Brendon to what little work he had to do, and took another of the colour-coded trails that followed a meandering line back in the direction of her café. This one was labeled Green Trail, and focused on the natural environment. For a while it led her past stands of local trees, then down to the river, where regular signboards—each needing a good clean and a touch up in places—told her about what kinds of birds and fish she might see in and around the water. Then, meandering through a forest glade, it came to a stop at a large, dirty greenhouse.

The sky was open above her, the beaming sun making the glass warm to the touch. Over the years it had done its work, though, leaving the inside of the glass murky with dark green algae. The trail clearly expected her to head inside, even though a chain barring entry had been hung across the door.

Bonnie walked to the corners of the greenhouse on either side, assessing its size and dimensions. It had a staggered roof, a central atrium rising in the middle to perhaps ten metres above her head, and sloping sides, like a Norman church, making it impossible to see the far end. Carefully planted trees along the outside left it camouflaged, which was why she probably hadn't noticed it before. Now, though, intrigued, she couldn't resist climbing over the chain, brushing away the weeds and pulling open the door.

A wave of heat hit her, along with the pungent scent of rotting plant matter. Inside, paths meandered through overgrown raised gardens displaying all manner of tropical plants, from tomatoes drowning in their own rotten produce to cacti and lemon trees still laden with shiny orange fruit. Some displays had suffered from a lack of maintenance, with the skeletons of unwatered plants standing lonely in dry flowerbeds, but others either had roots deep enough to find water or benefited from the mini ecosystem inside, where collected moisture dripped down from places along the roof.

Bonnie wandered the aisles, mouth agape, too stunned to voice her thoughts. Yet another of Christmas Land's neglected miracles, it was a tourist attraction in its own right, something that could be brought up to shining perfection with a bit of care and a few hours with a stepladder and a scrubbing brush.

And then, as she walked past a stand of cacti to find herself faced with the greenhouse's main attraction, she thought her jaw might hit the floor.

Standing in front of her beneath the raised central atrium, was a cacao tree. Large coco pods hung from bent branches, desperate to be picked. Bonnie reached out and gave one a tentative prod, before noticing the faded sign sticking out of the ground by the tree's foot.

As used in Mervin's Marshmallow Café!

So, it wasn't just the marshmallows that Mervin used natural, local ingredients for. He did the same for his hot chocolate. And if this was his tree, it made sense that he had looked after the entire bio-dome.

Bonnie sat down on a rickety wooden bench and gave a long sigh. Unable to resist a tired smile, she looked up at the cacao tree, hung heavy with pods, and wondered how she could turn one of those lumpy diamond-shaped pods into a steaming cup of hot chocolate.

22

LETTERS

Debbie was sitting on the terrace outside the pub, drinking a pint of stout and playing with her phone. As Bonnie took a seat opposite and sat down, Debbie looked up, a worried expression on her face.

'Phone's playing up,' she said. 'Might have to do a text run.'

'A what?'

'A run to some high ground, send some messages. It was working okay yesterday, after Shaun climbed up the phone mast and cut away the ivy, but it's on the blink now.'

'What happened?'

'I have some issues,' Debbie said.

Bonnie leaned forward, resting her chin on the backs of her hands. 'Tell Auntie Bonnie.'

Debbie gave a long, dramatic sigh. 'Like, basically, I've got Mitchell really wanting me to go back to Bristol, but I'm not sure I can go back to him right now. I need some time to myself.'

'Um, why?'

Debbie shook her head. 'I've broken up with Shaun,' she said.

'Already? You were with him, what, six hours?'

'Fourteen. Turned out he thought I was some singer from some metal band he liked, which, you know, is pretty flattering. When he found out I wasn't, he went kind of cold.' She shrugged. 'So I ended it.'

'Just like that?'

'I can't live up to being someone I'm not.' She took a long swallow of her drink. 'So, how was your day?'

Bonnie smiled. 'I've been doing my best to live up to being someone I'm not,' she said.

Debbie nodded, completely missing the irony. 'And how's it working out?'

'To be honest, it's been a breath of fresh air. This time last week I was all about running coupons for three-for-two on baked beans or apologising for selling out of PG Tips, but this week it's pulling up plants in marshes and trying to figure out how to turn a large, brown fruit into hot chocolate.'

Debbie leaned forward, narrowing her eyes. 'Morrico sold out of PG Tips?'

Bonnie shrugged. 'There's a guy who comes in whose daughter lives in Japan. He sends her out bulk loads. One day last month he bought nine boxes. I mean, we were only sold out for about five minutes, but you know. That's beside the point, though. I found a cacao tree.'

'What, like a real one?'

'Are there other kinds?' When Debbie just shrugged, Bonnie said, 'I think it belonged to Mervin. This place is crazier than I could ever have imagined.'

'Just imagine what it would be like if it was all fixed up.'

Bonnie sighed. 'That's the problem. That's all I can

imagine right now. I can't see anything else. It's like my whole past never existed and I was born the day we arrived here. All my old life feels like a bad dream and I've just woken up into what should actually be the dream. I have no idea what's going on.'

'Like a hall of mirrors?'

'What?'

'Like, you're seeing a whole bunch of yourself and you don't know which is the real one, so you're going kind of crazy?'

'Um, I suppose.'

Debbie grinned. 'So, what are you going to do?'

'Figure out how to make homemade hot chocolate, I suppose. Literally homemade.'

'That's awesome. Oh, and by the way, Mitchell said Barry's convinced his fiancée to have their wedding at Christmas Land. First week of December. Apparently Barry's totally loaded so it's going to be about a hundred people. At least.'

'Wow.'

'So, yeah. Oh, and my mum says it's totally okay for me to work for you. As long as you pay me and everything, and that I declare it so the family doesn't get blacklisted by social services.'

Bonnie took a deep breath. It felt like the deepest one she'd ever taken. 'Right,' she said. 'Let's get a shift on. Marshmallows don't make themselves.'

~

Debbie's plan to ascend the viewing tower in order to send a few text messages was thwarted by measure of it being closed, so she headed off to catch a lunchtime train into Quimbeck, leaving Bonnie to head back to the café alone.

Feeling overawed by the thought of opening the café, Bonnie decided now was the time to start getting to know her uncle a little better. Brewing a large pot of coffee, she took a steaming cup and carried it up the ladder to his office grotto.

It was as she had left it, piled high with papers, documents and letters. Bonnie took a seat and started to go through them one by one.

To her initial surprise, the café had been in rude health. Profit sheets and bank statements—the balance of which now passed to Bonnie, according to the lawyers' letter—showed a regular, consistent profit. However, unearthing several from previous years, she found that, while the café still did okay, it had been in gradual decline, probably due to the general malaise of the whole park.

Below the bank and tax documents, which she happily pushed aside, Bonnie found the document she had known she would find somewhere, but had been dreading: the closure letter.

Dear Leaseholder ("Merv" was scribbled alongside it),

It is with great regret that I write to inform you that Christmas Land will cease operation in the January following the date of this letter, unless by some stroke of luck its performance drastically increases. With almost all properties within the park owned by leaseholders such as yourself, there is no more money for investment, and sadly, a project begun fifty years ago will be put to rest. The magical lights of Christmas Land will go out for good.

It is with great regret that I have to write and send this letter. My heart is broken by doing so, but like everything in life, all good things come to an end, and Christmas Land is no exception. We should be proud of our history, of what we have achieved, of the magic we have shared. Unfortunately, we live in a world without magic, where no one looks further than their own hands, and beauty and joy are no longer truly appreciated. Christmas Land is a thing of the past, a thing belonging to a different generation which understood a different way of life.

So, the park that was my creation and my dream will close. Always the dreamer, I will allow you to continue trying to convince me otherwise up until the day the gates close for the last time.

I wish you all the best.

Yours, with great faith and regret,

S.N.

Bonnie frowned at the letter. Who on earth was S.N.? She had heard him—or her, maybe; Bonnie had no clue—referred to only as the Boss, but was that all anyone knew? The scribbed "Merv" at the top suggested her Uncle had been on friendly terms with their mysterious overlord, so perhaps Gene, or other older members of the park had been, too. It was worth asking, in case she could track the mysterious person down and appeal to them face to face.

She took a sip of her coffee, shook her head, and then began to go through the pile of correspondence she found beneath.

Half an hour later, she was still shaking her head, this time in disbelief, as she stared at the couple of dozen letters she had spread out on the table before her.

She also wore a smile. While she wouldn't quite say she felt jubilant, she felt very, very close.

About twenty-five people had gathered in the Mountain Breeze café. June and Niall were delivering plates of cookies and pitchers of fresh coffee to each table as Bonnie and Debbie entered. Bonnie immediately recognised several people, including Jason the reindeer handler, the three elves, Gene, in his woodland gear sitting with one huge, booted leg hooked over the other as he sucked on an empty pipe, and an old lady dressed rather like an Eskimo, whom Bonnie took to be Belinda.

Brendon came over to meet her, then introduced her to those people she hadn't yet met. Several were staff, others were leaseholders of various shops, restaurants, and attractions.

'Right, I think everyone who said they'd come is here,' Brendon said, leading Bonnie to a stool next to the café counter. 'Would you like me to say something first?'

Bonnie glanced across at Debbie, who had sat down next to Shaun and was passing him several CDs, whispering a few comments about each one. She smiled.

'No, I'll do it,' she said. Then, with her heart beating in her chest so loud she almost felt the need to shout, she clapped her hands together. 'Welcome, everyone,' she said. 'My name is Bonnie Green, as you probably know, since I just spoke with most of you. I'm Mervin Green's niece, and the beneficiary of his will.'

A few people murmured to their neighbours. Bonnie waited a few seconds before continuing.

'His will asked me to take over the café, but it was something I was reluctant about. You see, I'm not exactly one for rushing off on sudden adventures. In fact, my whole life has been quite the opposite. I've always quite avoided them, and well, in the end it got me nowhere. I live in a small semi-detached house in Weston super Mare, my grown up children don't speak to me, and I work in a supermarket.'

Murmurs passed through the crowd. Someone asked, 'Why did you call us to this meeting?'

'Well, I'm not familiar with how you do things,' Bonnie said. 'And I've seen the letter threatening to close the park in January—'

Several people stood up. Belinda, the diminutive Eskimo-dressed lady, shouted, 'It always gets better at Christmas. Always has done. Load of fuss over nothing. The park's going nowhere.'

'It sounds serious to me,' Bonnie said.

'Won't close,' shouted another older man, one Bonnie had been introduced to as Richard, owner of Russian Steppe Donuts and Milkshakes, a small café tucked into the restaurant forum area. 'We've been threatened before. Nothing happened. We had that letter three years ago, who remembers that?'

Brendon stood up. 'That was just a warning,' he said. 'That things needed to improve. We got a lot of snow that year, so tickets sold better. This is different.'

'Are you sure about that? And who are you, anyway,' Richard said, waving a hand at Bonnie, 'To start telling us what to do?'

Before Bonnie could reply, Gene stood up. At the sound of his huge suit shifting and his boots scraping on the floor, all other sound seemed to fade, until there was only the movement of Father Christmas as he made his way to the front.

Gene turned to face them, his head slowly moving back and forth until he had met every pair of eyes in the room. 'You want to know who this lady is? Well, I'll tell you.' He paused to wait for the whispers to stop. 'This lady here is customer zero.'

More murmurs. Gene nodded as he pulled something out of his pocket and held it up. A black and white photograph of three men, with an infant girl held in the arms of one.

'Three years old, she would have been,' Gene said, giving Bonnie an affectionate glance. 'That's me there, beside her dad, and that's Merv on the other side. The day the park opened. She was our test subject.' He glanced at Bonnie. 'I bet you barely remember it, do you?'

Bonnie wiped a tear from the corner of her eye. 'I had dreams ... and my dad used to talk about it as though it was a place we had once gone. And he said we'd go there again one day, but then he died....'

'You loved every second of it,' Gene said. 'Every ride, every stall, every character. I've never seen eyes so full of wonder. I knew then that the park would be a success, but that was a long time ago. We haven't moved with the times. We've let things go stale, let rides rust up and close down. People have moved out, locking up their shops and leaving. Sure, we've always had a sprinkling of customers, but fewer and fewer ever come back. What happened to the regulars we had twenty, thirty years ago? Every year we'd see the same faces, like old friends. And now....' He shook his head. 'How could we have let it get like this?'

'So what do we do?' called Jason.

Bonnie stepped forward. She reached into a bag and pulled out the bundle of letters she had found on Mervin's desk.

'My uncle had a plan,' she said. 'He had always kept in contact with his regular customers, and in his hour of need he had called them in, asking for their specialist help. Engineers to fix the rides, plumbers, builders, and electricians to repair the chalets, businessmen to figure out an action plan, lawyers to keep the park financed, even gardeners and stone masons to tidy up the flowerbeds and walkways. Painters, designers, mechanics … he had written letters to them all … but he died before he got a chance to mail them.'

Another murmur passed through the crowd. Someone asked, 'Are you going to send them?'

Bonnie turned the nearest one round. 'My friend picked up a bunch of stamps from Quim this afternoon. They're all ready to go. There's a mailbox by the station I'll be dropping them in tomorrow morning. Now, does anyone have any other ideas?'

Niall's hand shot up. 'We could create a mascot,' he said. Several people laughed, but others, coming around to the idea, nodded. 'How about a cutesy reindeer?'

Brendon nodded. 'It might work. Or how about we make character versions of all of us?'

The discussion moved back and forth. Someone else suggested creating golden tickets, special invites sent out to friends of friends, or even to people in the public sector who might help raise the profile of the park.

Debbie lifted her hand. 'You want to make this place sound better than it is?' she said. 'You have a customer limit anyway due to the environmental setting, so play up to it. Make it sound exclusive, like you're lucky because you're one in a thousand or whatever—'

'The limit is two thousand, five hundred at a time,' Brendon said.

'You don't tell them that,' Debbie said. 'If they want to go around and count, that's up to them. And create a waiting list. Give them something to look forward to. In three years time, we're going to Christmas Land! And damn well make it worth it when they arrive.'

The feeling in the room had shifted. Bonnie sensed a newfound sense of positivity, of hope. 'We start tomorrow,' she said. 'We'll begin by cleaning and tidying up the park. We can do this, I know we can.'

As Brendon stepped up to formally end the meeting, he turned to Bonnie. 'I'd just like to say, on behalf of everyone here, welcome to the Christmas Land family.'

Bonnie smiled. 'Thank you,' she said. 'I think I'm going to enjoy it.'

PART II
A MAGICAL AWAKENING

23

GOLDEN TICKETS

'Bonnie! Are you sure you're safe up there?'

Bonnie, hanging on with one hand to a branch as she reached out with the other to grab a cacao pod hanging out over the floor some five metres below, glanced down at Debbie, bizarrely wearing a reindeer-design jumper under her trench-coat. A strand of red and white streamer wound its way through her otherwise black braids: it was as far as she would go by way of concession.

'I'm fine,' Bonnie said, even as one foot slipped from the crux of the tree and briefly scrabbled in open air. 'Never felt better. I'll just get this last one—'

She stretched, her fingers closing over the pod. With a twist it came loose.

'Got it.'

'Now get down.'

'I'm coming.'

A couple of minutes later, Bonnie stood beside Debbie on the floor below the atrium. The sun streamed through windows cleaned and polished over the last couple of weeks. Already newly planted flowers and bushes were beginning to show signs of taking to their new homes. Plans were in place to assign a new head botanist and design a walking tour. Of course, the Pohutukawa tree which stood at one end of the atrium, known as the New Zealand Christmas tree because of its beautiful red hue, would be one of the main attractions. After a photo opportunity, customers would be directed to Mervin's Marshmallow Café for a free hot chocolate made with homegrown cacao.

Outside, a group of stonemasons were at work repairing the cobbled walkway that lead from the main circular path down to the greenhouse. Bonnie gave them a wave and invited them in for a drink when they were finished.

'So, how many came?' Debbie asked. 'Out of all those letters you sent?'

Bonnie smiled. 'Almost all of them. Uncle Mervin had made some friends over the years, it seems.'

They passed a shop called Bad Taste Christmas Goods. A young boy was outside, polishing the windows, while through an open door, an older couple were arranging goods on shelves. Debbie gave her jumper a sheepish pat.

'Figured it would only be right to be their first customer,' she said. 'Not sure I'd wear this round town, but it seems to fit in all right here.'

'I'm glad to hear it. Are you ready for a coffee?'

'Bingo.'

They headed across to the Mountain Breeze, where they found Niall on duty. When they asked after June, the boy told them she was next door, cleaning the adjacent shop. New stock was due to arrive the following day, so they needed somewhere to put it.

'So, we have one more week,' Debbie said, glancing up at a promotional poster on the wall behind the counter.

'December 5th. What's that, one month since we arrived? It's nothing, is it? Are you scared?'

Bonnie smiled. 'I'm trying not to let myself be, but I'm terrified. I quit my job over this. The Old Ragtag delighted in telling me I wouldn't be welcomed back, and if I had a change of heart I'd have to reapply. The old sod even told me my age would likely count against me.'

'Isn't that illegal?'

'Technically, of course. But he knows me. He knows how old I am.'

'You're not old.'

Bonnie patted Debbie on the arm. 'That's nice of you to say. To be honest, the longer I stay here, the younger I feel.'

'That's nice.' Debbie frowned. 'The longer I'm here, the less Goth I feel. That's a big concern.'

'What are you going to do about it?'

'Next time I can get wi-fi, I'm going to order some of those sunglasses that show everything in black and white. That'll be a good start.'

'Sounds fun.'

'And Shaun and me are going to start a metal band.'

'Really?'

Debbie nodded. 'Shaun plays bass. Apparently Jason the reindeer guy can play drums. We just need a guitarist.'

'So, you're the singer?'

'Of course.'

'I can't wait to hear it.'

Debbie grinned. 'Thinking to set up a residency in the club. Once a week. We'll basically thrash it out, then play a couple of metal Christmas-song covers just to stay on topic.'

'Sounds perfect.'

The door opened, and June came in. Seeing Bonnie

and Debbie, she came over. 'Good news,' she said. 'I just heard from Brendon. We got a donation from a renewable energy company. They're sending a team to inspect the park for the possibility of the installation of solar panels, to see if it's viable. They should be here by Wednesday.'

'That's great,' Bonnie said. 'If we can have them up and running by Christmas, it'll surely save the park money.'

'They told Brendon that it's possible the park could generate one hundred percent of its own electricity.'

'Perfect.'

As June went off to help Niall, Bonnie couldn't help basking in a little success. After several meetings with the other leaseholders, they had come to the conclusion to push the environmental theme as much as possible, reinventing Christmas Land as an environmentally sustainable and low impact theme park. All food was to be locally sourced, all products fair-trade or cottage-industry produced, as much as possible recycled, everything energy efficient, and where possible, new construction was to be carried out with recycled material.

So far, it was working well, and the park had attracted national attention. Temporarily closed to visitors, it was open only to registered journalists, some of whom were regularly seen wandering about, asking questions and taking pictures.

Whether it would translate into ticket sales, Bonnie didn't know. She could only hope, otherwise by the end of January she would be homeless. She still had her house in Weston super Mare, of course, but she had rented it out and the tenants had a one-year lease. The rent was enough to give her a small profit over the cost of the mortgage, but it wasn't enough to rent something else, and without a job, she would need a sofa to sleep on.

'Stop brooding,' Debbie said. 'We're game on. No way the Boss is going to shut the park after all this community effort.'

'I hope not,' Bonnie said. 'It would be easier if we knew who it was, in order that we could appeal to him directly.'

'Just trust me, it'll be fine. So, who are you going to send your golden tickets to?'

The idea of handing out exclusive tickets had been a popular one. Each member of staff had been given five tickets to hand out to whomever they chose. The condition was that each ticket was valid for a three-night stay for up to a family of four, bookable when space was available. Each ticket came with a hundred-pound voucher to be used on drinks, entertainment, or in any shop of their choice. The theory behind it was that once here, customers would spend lots of additional money, while giving a favourable review of the park to anyone who would listen, word-of-mouth being by far the best advertising.

'I haven't quite decided,' Bonnie said. 'I'm going to give one to Jean from work, because she was always nice to me, and I feel bad about leaving her behind. And I thought I'd give one to my old boss, you know, just so he can come up here and see how much better off I am.'

'Come on, you know that's not the reason. Gloating isn't you, Bon.'

Bonnie shrugged. 'All right, I suppose I just wanted to offer an olive branch. And he was always so miserable at work, who knows what kind of a personal life he has. I thought it might be nice to cheer him up a little.'

'That's very charitable of you.'

'And my kids.'

Debbie lifted an eyebrow. 'Steve and Claire?'

Bonnie sighed. 'I can't hate them, you know? They're my children.'

'They both took Phil's side. I'm surprised you didn't burn every picture you have of them.'

'One day you might understand,' Bonnie said. 'They'd have to commit murder before I'd disown them. And even then, it would be hard.'

Debbie patted her on the hand. 'You're a saint,' she said. 'If I told Mum that Dad had run off because she dressed like a potato and was as boring as washing up, I'd expect to get kicked out.'

Bonnie rolled her eyes. 'They didn't say that. Not those exact words, anyway. And I know your mum. She wouldn't throw you out.'

'She might.'

'She wouldn't. I never threw my kids out. They had both already moved out. Yeah, they said some pretty hurtful things, but I don't think they knew the whole story. I always put on a face for them, you know. I knew what Phil was doing, but I never let it show. And I had a house to run. I had food to put on the table, cleaning to do, money to earn, since our savings always seemed to be shrinking. I was a fool, I know I was, but I did it for them.'

'I wish you were my mum,' Debbie said. 'Well, at least my second mum. My first one is decent enough.'

'I am. Who was it who carried you up the stairs last week?'

'Ah, you were just being a mate. And I would have made it eventually. Me and Alan got on the sherry. I'm not used to granny drinks.'

'Alan?'

'Ah, we're just mates.'

Bonnie smiled. 'I'm glad you have friends. Right, we

need to get back to the café. I want another go at turning those lumps of tree into hot chocolate.'

As they headed back across the plaza, the hum of machinery around them, Bonnie thought about the golden tickets tucked into an envelope in the café's kitchen. She knew Jean would be delighted, and even the Old Ragtag might crack a rare smile. But she worried about the others. What would Steve and Claire say? Claire, off backpacking across Africa or somewhere, probably wouldn't come, but Steve, living in Swindon with his wife and young son—a grandson Bonnie had rarely met, and not at all in the last eighteen months—would have no excuse. Little Timothy would love the reindeer and the fairground rides. If they chose not to come, it would be a greater rejection than any other.

24

SNOW

'Hi, Bonnie,' Len said, smiling as she pulled up a stool and sat down. 'I was beginning to think you weren't coming back.'

Bonnie smiled. 'I'm afraid I decided to stay after all. Here, I brought you these.' She reached into a bag at her feet and pulled out a paper bag and a sealed plastic container.

'What have you got for me?'

She pushed the paper bag across the bar. 'A present. A fresh batch of marshmallows.' She grinned. 'Try them and tell me I'm not getting better.'

'They were fantastic before.'

'Ah, last time I had the sugar content totally wrong, and I didn't whisk the egg enough so it tasted more like a lump of plastic than a marshmallow.'

'I thought they tasted great.'

'You're just being nice.'

'My son was visiting, so I gave one to him, and he said the same,' Len said. 'Only one, mind. And Young Bill, my oldest and most regular customer, he had a little taste.'

At the end of the bar, a grizzled man wearing a green parka jacket raised a hand and gave Bonnie a gap-toothed smile. 'Divine,' he said, before turning back to his pint.

'You're onto a winner with these,' Len said. 'What's in the other bag?'

Bonnie gave a sheepish grin. 'Well, I was wondering if I could offer you a little business preposition.'

'Oh?'

'This is some homemade hot chocolate mix. Off the tree in Christmas Land. I concocted it myself. Plus some sugar and cinnamon out of the shops here in Quim. Totally local.'

'You want me to drink it?'

'And if you like it well enough, I want you to sell it.'

'Here?'

'Why not?'

'This is a pub.'

Bonnie pointed at a coffee machine behind the bar. 'You sell coffee, and I know you do hot chocolate, because I've seen you carrying it outside.'

Len shrugged. 'But that's just packet stuff.'

'Exactly. I want you to sell my stuff, and tell people where it comes from.'

'And what do I get out of it?'

'Money. You can sell it for however much you like, and hopefully I'll get a few more customers up in Christmas Land. We're only allowed a certain number of overnight visitors, but day visitors are also important.'

Len grimaced. 'Christmas Land. Huh. I'll think about it.'

'We're undergoing a few changes,' she said. 'I'm pretty sure you'd like it.'

'Haven't been up there since I was a kid, and it was tacky even then.'

'In the last month alone, we've had a ton of investment. There are plans for an interactive Nordic museum, which will focus on Scandinavian culture to carry the park through the summer months. We've contacted schools all over the region about visits, and had a good response. Christmas Land is sticking around, whether you stuck up types here in Quim like it or not.'

'We're not stuck up.'

'Yes, you are. All "look at us in our posh little Lake District village."' Bonnie grinned, impressed with her own impression.

'You haven't grown up with the tackiest theme park in England just five miles up the road,' Len said.

'It's not tacky anymore. Well, it won't be soon, once we reopen.'

'I suppose I'll have to force myself to visit sometime.'

Bonnie reached into a pocket of her coat and pulled out an envelope. 'Now you have no choice,' she said.

'What's this?'

'Open it and find out.'

Len lifted an eyebrow as he opened the envelope and slid out the golden piece of paper. 'Huh? "Grants the holder three nights in the world's only Christmas-themed amusement park",' he read. 'What?'

'You could bring your wife and son,' Bonnie said, getting up from the stool and picking up her bag.

'My....' Len was still staring at the ticket. 'Um, thanks.'

'I look forward to seeing you there,' Bonnie said, flashing Len a smile as she headed for the door. 'Be sure to come by for some marshmallows and hot chocolate.'

~

It felt good to have a purpose. Until she had made the final decision to take on Mervin's café, basic survival had been Bonnie's main aim. Getting through the day without losing her job, her house, or her health, there had been nothing to look forward to other than her cornflakes the next morning, and hopefully a chat with Jean over whatever was on the front page of the day's newspapers.

Her new role still felt unfamiliar, but she was growing into it. At first, telling people what to do had felt strange, but after reading through the letters Uncle Mervin had prepared but never had time to send, she realised there was no other choice. Her uncle's enthusiasm and drive to save the park which had become his home couldn't be ignored.

Back at Christmas Land, she found a team painting and repairing the gates, filling in potholes in the approaching path, and repairing holes in the perimeter fence. Brendon, dressed in overalls, spotted her and waved.

'Good news,' he said, as she wandered over. 'Safety standards officials just gave the green light to the Christmas Land Coaster. It's been years since that old thing ran, but we're about to see it operating again.' He smiled. 'Thanks to a group of your uncle's friends.'

'I guess his marshmallows must really have been something,' Bonnie said. 'If mine are half as good, I'll be happy. Is everyone ready for the café's official reopening party tonight?'

'As soon as we're done here, we'll be right over,' Brendon said.

Bonnie smiled. Aware she had a lot of preparation to do, she headed back to Ings Forest station and skirted the lake until she came to the fenced area where Mervin's mallow plants grew. With only a tiny yard at the back of her house in Weston, gardening was something else she had needed to learn. With the help of a couple of the park's resident caretakers, she had sectioned off the patch of marshland by plant size, with one area reserved for newly planted seedlings.

Among his belongings in the grotto, Bonnie had found a notebook, in which Uncle Mervin had kept a rough diary, along with a list of recipes he was working on. Local Mallow was only one of his recipes, with others coming from all over the world. She discovered he'd had a fascination with mountain blends, with Himalayan Mallow, Andean Mallow, and even Kilimanjaro Coffee Blend Mallow all appearing on his menus. Bonnie had managed to hunt down a list of suppliers and ask them to resume their service.

The garden was looking good. She waded into the water and selected a couple of roots, amazed at how easy it now seemed. Then, after tucking them into a plastic bag, she headed back to the park. She was nearly at the gates when she saw something floating gently down through the air.

A snowflake.

She stuck out a hand and it nestled briefly on her palm before melting away. Bonnie stared at where it had been, then looked up, realising others were falling around her, the air filling with a light, feathery curtain of snow.

25

COASTER

THE CHRISTMAS LAND COASTER WAS MORE OF A SCENIC ride than an out-and-out thriller of a rollercoaster, but as Brendon interrupted the café's opening party to announce that it was ready for its inaugural reopening ride, Bonnie couldn't ignore a shiver of excitement. It's curving metal rails were visible all over the park as it twisted and turned through the trees overhead, making sharp cutbacks and at one point dipping down into an underground tunnel before reemerging a couple of hundred metres away. With a tall fence protecting the entrance and exit, Bonnie had no clue what was down there, nor did she know where it went when it arced outside of the park grounds and disappeared into the forest, before reappearing again near the station at the very rear of the park.

While the rails were out in the open, the trucks had always been hidden away in a shed behind the station. Now, sat on gleaming, freshly polished rails, they were a series of mini sleigh designs, with the front locomotive designed to look like a pair of reindeer.

Waiting with the rest of the assembled staff, Bonnie

was about to climb into a cart near the back when Brendon raised his hand and waved her over.

'No, come up here, please, Bonnie. This old thing would still be rusted solid if it wasn't for you.'

'I've never been on a rollercoaster before,' she said, reluctantly heading to the front.

Brendon waved her into the first car, right behind the reindeer. Gingerly, Bonnie climbed into the seat. Brendon climbed in beside her and pulled down the safety bar.

'Let's see how the old girl goes, shall we?' he said. 'I'm afraid work hasn't finished on some of the displays, but we're getting there.'

With everyone in their seats, the coaster began to move. Slowly at first, it rose up a slight incline towards a dipping corner. Bonnie, who had never been on a rollercoaster in her life, clung to the safety bar with all her might, terrified it would suddenly give way and throw them out into oblivion. As the coaster crept up the incline towards the first drop, she was certain she was about to die, be sick, or both.

'Relax,' Brendon said, laughing. 'It's pretty tame.'

'I'm trying,' Bonnie said through gritted teeth. 'I haven't been this scared since I was last in a car with my maniac daughter driving.'

'If it's anything like June's,' Brendon said, turning to wink at his wife in the seat behind, 'I imagine this will be tame in comparison.'

'Watch it up there,' June said. 'Remember who controls what you eat.'

'Sorry, love,' Brendon said, as June gave him a lighthearted thump on the back, causing a distorted groan of piped music.

'And don't forget to change your batteries before we open.'

Brendon looked about to reply, but the coaster suddenly dropped, throwing them all back in their seats. Bonnie was too scared even to cry out as they hurtled into a sweeping bend before passing through a series of dips and rises. On the last, they passed a display of reindeer-shaped marionettes standing around among a forest of plastic trees devoid of fake snow.

Brendon grimaced. 'Haven't finished the reindeer forest yet, then,' he muttered. 'Better get another team on that soon.'

They swung around another corner and into a terrifying drop. Up ahead was only darkness, the underground tunnel.

'The dwarf mines,' Brendon said, sounding a lot more distressed than he had before they began. 'Where they mine all the goods for the Christmas presents.'

Protected from the elements underground, the display of little marionettes working in a mine while singing Christmas songs was in better working order than the previous one, even though a few light-bulbs needed replacing. Bonnie smiled at the colourful carts moving through the brightly lit display, loaded with glittering jewels.

Then they were rushing back up into the daylight, cutting around a corner, and passing along a flat section passing over the main plaza. Mervin's Marshmallow Café, with its freshly painted walls and glowing sign stood to one side. Bonnie smiled, glancing up at the windows of the upstairs flat which was now hers, and the rooftop, with its secret patio, carefully concealed to be hidden from the coaster's riders. It had been nearly a month, and Bonnie could still hardly believe how easy it all felt. By now, the tenants would have moved into her house in Weston. Aside from a couple of phone calls from the letting agency, she had heard nothing, and had barely even thought about it. Here among the trees of Christmas Land, with its gradually declining temperatures and light dustings of morning snow, she felt more at home than ever.

The coaster jerked around another corner. Twenty metres below, the reindeer wandered around their enclosure, some of them picking at a food trough, others rubbing their antlers against a couple of scratching posts.

'Here we go,' Brendon said. 'The enchanted forest.'

'Where?'

'We're leaving the park. At least the main part of it.'

The coaster passed over the top of the perimeter fence, cutting through trees which had been allowed to grow up around it, creating a leafy avenue just over their heads. Its speed slowed to allow them to enjoy the scenery, then it carved around an outcrop of rock and passed through a narrow, rocky valley. By now Bonnie had no clue where they were. As it began to slow again, she wondered if they were about to break down. She was just about to voice her fears to Brendon when the valley opened out, and the coaster cruised past a little log cabin hidden in the forest. Outside, a model of Father Christmas lifted a hand and waved, his head nodding from side to side. Beside him, a reindeer missing one side of its antlers lifted its nose and gave a sudden snort.

'Need to get someone out to fix that,' Brendon said. 'Otherwise, it's looking okay.'

'Where are we?'

'Father Christmas's Cabin,' Brendon said. 'In the winter, we do guided forest walks out here. There's an entrance on the other side, and inside the cabin is a little grotto with comfy chairs where you can get hot chocolate and mince pies. At least, we used to. It's been closed for about six years.'

'I'd suggest you get it open as quickly as possible.'

'We're working on it. By Christmas, if we have all hands on deck.'

The coaster angled back through the forest, its speed slowly increasing. Bonnie turned to Brendon, one hand closing over his arm.

'What's going on?'

Brendon grinned. 'Oh, you didn't think it was all gentle and safe, did you?'

The passengers began to murmur nervously. Bonnie looked ahead through the trees, to where the rails appeared to lift vertically in front of them.

'Oh my—'

They were through the loop almost as soon as they hit it, but for a couple of brief seconds, Bonnie felt her life flash before her eyes. Then they were gliding gently into the station as people simultaneously gasped with fright and cheered. They came to a stop and the safety bars lifted. Bonnie turned to look for Debbie as she got out. Her friend had been seated a couple of rows behind her, and as they hit the loop, Debbie's cry had been by far the loudest.

'I wasn't scared!' Debbie snapped at Jason, as the reindeer handler laughed. 'I swallowed a butterfly or a spider or something. That's all. Don't look at me like that. I could do it again right now, but I think I should let someone else have a go, don't you?'

Bonnie glanced at the waiting line, which currently numbered only Belinda, who had decided, due to her advanced age, to sit the ride out.

'What did you think?' Brendon asked, as June and Niall crowded around.

Bonnie smiled. 'Fantastic,' she said. 'I think I need a hot chocolate and a marshmallow to calm my nerves, though. Party's on for anyone who wants to come.'

26

THE MYSTERY

Bonnie set the tray of marshmallows down on the table with a slightly louder thump than usual. Debbie, staring out of the window, jerked her head around.

'Any chance of getting some help this morning?' Bonnie said. 'I don't want to be the dragon manager or anything, but it would be nice to have someone perhaps take the chairs down off the tables.'

Debbie sighed. 'All right.' Like something in a liquid state, she started to rise, one arm pushing her body up while her legs seemed to stay behind.

Bonnie grinned. 'Worried about Mitchell showing up?'

'How did you know?'

'Because they're due today, aren't they? The whole wedding party and all that? Another reason why I'd really love some help with these marshmallows. I need to make about another thousand, and my arms are killing me.'

'Sorry,' Debbie said, standing up. 'It's just that I've never been in a love triangle before.'

'I thought you said Shaun and you had broken up?'

'Well, I lent him some CDs, and he's all like, we have

the exact same music tastes. Like, we were separated at birth.'

'Isn't that a bit weird?'

'He meant cloned or something, not like brother and sister.'

'I'm still finding that weird.'

Debbie shrugged. 'I don't know. I mean, he's cool, but I don't know if I want to be bogged down in a relationship with someone who lives around the corner, and who dresses like an elf and does that weird little jig for a living.'

'As opposed to a deaf metal drummer?' Bonnie laughed. 'That wasn't meant as a joke.'

'Mitchell works in HSBC. He's an accounts manager. That's cool and everything, but I can't do the corporate dog thing. I'm a liberal.'

'Right.'

'I can't go against my beliefs, just for the sake of a man.'

'Nope.'

'I mean, it's tempting, but I'm torn.'

'Like that girl from *Neighbours*?'

Debbie rolled her eyes. 'I forgot that you were young in the nineties.'

'I wasn't that young. Younger. My kids used to watch it.'

Debbie looked up. 'Did either of them respond to your letters?'

Bonnie shook her head. 'Not yet. Claire, I can understand. Who knows where she is right now. Last time I checked her social media she was in Russia. Steve, though … I thought he might have got back to me.'

'Maybe he's just busy.'

'Maybe.'

The bell above the door went. Gene, dressed down by

his standards in a brown Medieval smock and a leather waistcoat over trousers than looked hand-woven out of cord, stepped inside, then waved someone in after him.

'Ladies, good day to you. I just wanted to introduce you to Ben.'

The young man was about thirty, with light brown hair and dark, hazelnut brown eyes. When he smiled Bonnie felt a sense of peace inside. Dragging her eyes away from him, she glanced at Debbie, who was staring wide-eyed.

'My grandson,' Gene said. 'He's raw, but he's keen. Aren't you, lad?'

'It's very nice to meet you,' Ben said. 'I'm looking forward to seeing you around.'

'I'm getting too old for this gig,' Gene said. 'At least the more active parts of it. Each time the kids treat me like a tree I feel something pop. The lad here's got a bit more life in him. I'll be stepping back, sitting on the porch a lot more.'

'I can't believe this place even exists,' Ben said. 'It's amazing.'

'We think so too,' Bonnie said.

Debbie was still staring.

'Debs?' Bonnie said.

'What's your favorite Judas Priest album?' Debbie said, in a startling monotone.

'Screaming for Vengeance,' Ben said without hesitation. 'Although I know most people go for Painkiller.'

Debbie gave a slow nod. 'Awesome,' she said.

Gene frowned at Bonnie, eyebrows so thick they almost covered his eyes. Bonnie just smiled. 'Be sure to stop by for some marshmallows,' she said. 'We have the best around here.'

'Thanks,' Ben said. Then, turning to Debbie, he added, 'I'll see you around?'

'Sure.'

As they left, Bonnie started laughing. 'Should we make it a love-square?'

'Are you making coffee? I think I need to sit down.'

~

After lunch, leaving Debbie to continue with the marshmallows, Bonnie took a walk around the park. She had made it her policy not to overwork herself, making sure she spent plenty of time out in the fresh air, something she had rarely done in Weston, even with the seafront just a short walk away. If she was going to change her life, she was going to do it the right way, and not just switch one stressful situation for another.

Stopping by the restaurant forum to see how work was going on a paint job for the building's ceiling, she found Brendon sitting outside Russian Steppes Donuts and Milkshakes. She ordered a drink from Richard and went out onto the patio to join Brendon. He was peering into a laptop computer, and looked up with a smile as she approached.

'We just got another booking,' he said. 'Someone's cashed in one of your golden tickets. A Mr. Cyril Reeves?'

Bonnie couldn't help but laugh. 'The Old Ragtag! He actually used it.' At Brendon's confused expression, she added, 'Sorry, that's my old boss. He was a right old scrooge and a general pain in the bum. I sent him one as a kind of peace offering.'

'Well, he's booked over the wedding weekend.'

'I'd better make sure to mop my floors twice every morning,' Bonnie said. 'He's a clean freak. Always used to make us clean everything twice. Drove us mad, he did.'

'Did you give out the rest of your tickets?'

Bonnie nodded. 'No takers yet?'

'Not yet. We're nearly full for opening week, though. This is going to be incredible.'

'Do you think we'll get a stay of execution, or will the mysterious owner pull the plug anyway?'

Brendon shook his head. 'We can but hope.'

'And you have no idea who it could be?'

'None. In all the time I've been here, I never heard anything about the park's owner until that letter came.'

Bonnie frowned. 'Isn't there some way I could find out?'

'No idea. When we saw the lease for the Mountain Breeze advertised, we just went with the hundred year thing. Never thought it could get pulled out from under us, and until last year, we'd barely even thought about it.'

'That's the general problem. Everyone burying their heads.'

'Well, thanks to you, we've got another chance.'

'Thanks to my uncle. All I did was post his letters.'

'And a good job you did.'

Bonnie decided to leave him to his work. Giving herself another twenty minutes before she had to get back and relieve Debbie, she took a meandering walk around the back of the park, past the reindeers, and through an area set aside for older customers. The low building had a small heated swimming pool which was now open again for three hours every morning and evening, as well as a wide seating area for relaxing, and a small library, mostly filled with books on local history.

Bonnie, unsure quite what she was thinking, headed inside. With the park still closed to customers, the building was empty except for its resident custodian, another long-term park resident called Louis Vierstein. Bonnie found him pottering around in the lobby, dusting off bunches of plastic flowers. She asked him if there were any books in the library on the park's history, and after a shrug, Louis directed her to a corner shelf.

Judging by the coating of dust, the books looked rarely if ever read. Bonnie took one down and carried it to a table, wincing at the grime on her finger after wiping it along the spine. A general book about local history, the pages inside were crisp and almost stuck together. Bonnie turned them slowly, one at a time, peering at black and white photographs of local mines and quarries, half-built cottages, lakeside piers, horse-drawn carts, early tractors, wide, grainy Lake District landscapes, and lines of felled trees stacked up for logging.

One by one, she skim-read the captions, hoping for some clue. She turned a page with a picture showing the opening of a bank in Quimbeck, and then … nothing.

Her fingers lifted the shredded triangle at the bottom of a torn out page. The beginning of a caption read: *the founders, at the breaking of the ground on the Christmas Land proj—*.

The picture was missing. Frowning, Bonnie felt along the tear, but there was no clue as to how long ago the picture had been torn out. It could be days or years, decades, even.

The founders….

She closed the book, putting it to one side, and hunted for more, but while she came across several other local history books, she found no other mention of Christmas Land.

She took the first book and went to see Louis, but the old man just shrugged. 'No one much looks in that section,' he said. 'Page there could have been torn before you was born.'

'You have no idea who might have taken it?'

'Nope.'

'And you have no idea who these founders were?'

'None. I arrived in seventy-four. Park had been open a few years by then.'

'And you've never heard of anyone with the initials S.N?'

'Nope. Never met him, never seen him. Never heard from him neither until that letter arrived last summer.'

'You got one too?'

'Yeah, course. I own a stake in the pub. Twenty-percent.'

'Do you mind if I borrow this book?'

'Nope, so long as you bring it back.'

∼

Back home at the café, Bonnie let Debbie off on a break and a hung an OUT TO LUNCH sign over the front door to make sure she wasn't disturbed. Then, she took the book upstairs, made a coffee, and sat down on the sofa to study it further.

No matter how hard she looked, though, the picture was still gone. She had wondered whether it might have been torn out by accident and slipped inside the dust jacket for safekeeping, but it was nowhere to be found. Definitely stolen, she concluded, to hide the group's identity.

After finishing her coffee, she headed upstairs to Mervin's grotto, and searched his bookcase for another copy of the book, but found nothing. There were a few other books on local history, however, but on flipping through them, she found the same thing: any mention of Christmas Land was suspicious by its absence. Bonnie shook her head, mystified. It was as though the park ceased to exist the moment you boarded the train at Ings Forest station.

Muffled through the floor, she heard Debbie coming up the stairs and hurried down to meet her. Debbie looked flustered, her cheeks glowing.

'What happened?'

'Sorry, just took in a lunchtime pint,' Debbie said.

Bonnie frowned. 'You're supposed to be on duty.'

'Yeah, but we're not open yet, are we?'

Bonnie laughed. 'I'll let it go this time. Anything interesting happen in the pub?'

'For once, no.' Suddenly noticing the book Bonnie was holding, Debbie frowned. 'Doing some swatting up?' she asked.

Bonnie explained her mission to find the missing photograph, and her growing suspicion that someone in the park might have taken it.

Debbie waited until she'd finished, then said, 'Easy way to find out. Here, let me see.'

Bonnie passed Debbie the book. Debbie opened it to the title page and pointed at some small print at the bottom.

'The publisher,' she said. 'See if they're still operating, and if so, ask if they have any copies in print. Failing that, go down to Quim and see if there's a local library. Bet you there is. Bound to have a copy, aren't they? Probably collecting dust in a corner somewhere.'

Bonnie mentally brought up the train times to Quim in her head. 'Do you think you could watch the café for me for a few hours?'

Debbie lifted an eyebrow. 'From the inside or from the window of the pub?'

Bonnie laughed. 'You can have the afternoon off, so

anyway you choose. I'll be back later, unless I miss the last train.'

Debbie grinned. 'Give me a call if you end up having to walk back. I'll get Jason to go and get you with the sleigh.'

27

PAPER TRAIL

During the short train ride Bonnie searched for the book's publisher on her mobile phone's internet application. Unsurprisingly, the company had long ago gone out of business, leaving her with no choice but to hope a copy of the book was stocked somewhere. On a bookseller website she found the book listed for the extortionate price of five hundred pounds, but when Bonnie clicked to check availability, it was listed as out of stock.

In Quimbeck, she headed to the town centre where she knew there was a local map. She found the library, but when she arrived, she almost thumped the door with frustration. A sign hung in the window: closed on Tuesdays and Thursdays

With a couple of hours to kill before the next train, she wandered up and down the little high street. Most shops were decorated for Christmas, with quaint displays of local ornaments and trinkets. Bonnie picked up a couple of things that would look nice in the café's windows, even stopping to order a couple of dozen hand-carved reindeer figurines she thought would make pretty table ornaments. The craft shop lady told her to return in a week, handing her a receipt.

She still had a little time left to kill, and thought about walking along the river, but when she came out of the shop it had begun to rain. On the stroke of six o'clock, most shops were closing, and even though the town looked delightful with Christmas lights strung across the streets, the only shelter on offer besides the cold train station waiting room were the expensive local restaurants or a pub.

She headed for The King's Thistle. Len gave her a wide smile, but looked disappointed that she hadn't brought him any fresh marshmallows. He held up an empty hot chocolate bag and asked if he could order more.

'I had one lady drink four on the trot,' he said. 'I was going to limit her at five to save some for other customers, but she had to run to catch a train. Told me she'd be back around Christmas with her Women's Institute group, so I need a couple more bags as soon as you can manage it.'

'I'm glad it's popular,' Bonnie said, trying to sound modest, but secretly beaming inside. She had tweaked the recipe a dozen times, but still wasn't confident. Debbie, of course, told her everything was lush, but Debbie was far too easily pleased. 'We're not yet open up in Christmas Land, so I don't know how it'll go down.'

'Extremely well, I imagine,' Len said. 'That stuff is like gold dust. I don't know how you managed it.'

'A lot of messing around,' Bonnie said.

She ordered a drink and took up a stool at the bar.

'I'm sorry not to have booked anything with that ticket you kindly gave me,' Len said, as he set her drink down. 'I did mention it to my son, and he sounded keen, but I'm not sure I can take the time off with the

Christmas rush. Quim gets a lot of business through December.'

'Maybe save it until the spring,' Bonnie said.

'Won't that be a bit strange, celebrating Christmas in the spring?'

'We're working on that,' Bonnie said. 'We're trying to change the image of Christmas Land into something more along the lines of an ecological park with a Christmas theme.'

'Sounds … odd.'

'It'll work if we get it right,' she said, thinking about the many meetings she had sat through where they discussed the various classes and tours they could provide, focusing on the environment as well as promoting Scandinavian culture as a backdrop to the modern Christmas fairytale. 'I've never been involved in anything like this before, and it's so exciting.'

'It sounds it. What brought you down to Quim, anyway? A bit of Christmas shopping?'

Bonnie had almost forgotten the book. She pulled her copy out of her bag and passed it over to Len.

'I found this in the library at Christmas Land,' she said. 'Unfortunately there's a page missing. I came down to Quim to see if they have another copy in the library here.'

Len flicked through a few pages. 'I'm sure they will have,' he said. 'This missing page is important, is it?'

'It might be,' Bonnie said. 'I'm trying to find out who owns the park, and if possible contact them. It seems to be a big secret. The missing page probably identified the person, and someone ripped it out to keep their identity secret.'

'Why would they do something like that?'

'I have no idea.'

They made small talk for a while. Bonnie shared her

progress up at the park, while Len talked enthusiastically about his son, Thomas, who was in the fourth year of a dentistry degree, and would be coming home for the Christmas holidays in a week. In return, Bonnie found herself talking about Steve and Claire. She tried to remain positive, but eventually Len noticed the change in tone.

'Something happened with them, didn't it?'

Bonnie sighed. 'They took my ex-husband's side during the divorce. I never wanted to talk ill of him in front of them, but he was such a manipulator, and would say all kinds of things about me. He could put on any kind of face, and when it all went down he painted himself as the hardworking husband with the inattentive wife, and they swallowed everything. Didn't matter that I was working all hours at Morrico because he was spending our savings on his flings, or that he eventually ran off with someone else. They just took his side. They were both off at university by then so there was no wrangling over custody or child support. It was a simple matter of opinion, and they sided with him. Steve was so angry with me, we didn't speak for a year. Even now I'm lucky to get a phone call every six months. Claire is a bit different. She's got her father in her; his sense of adventure. Whereas his was finding his way into as many bedrooms as possible, hers is wandering across the world. I get the odd postcard, but that's about it.'

Len sighed. 'You never know how they're going to turn out,' he said. 'You do your best, and they reject you. I'll never know how lucky I got with Thomas. I did my best, but living in a pub, I was always working evenings. I always took weekends off for my boy, but I was certain he'd end up rejecting me or blaming me for something. In the end, though, he turned out as fine as I could have hoped.' He shrugged. 'Pot luck, I suppose. Another drink?'

Bonnie realised she had finished the sherry. She glanced at her watch. 'I have to run,' she said. 'We're only a few days away from the grand re-opening. I have reindeer signs to paint and weeds to pull up.'

'Good luck. Stop by anytime, and let me know when you can get me another hot chocolate supply. I'll make it worth your while.'

'Thanks!'

Bonnie headed out into the dark. Quim was all lit up by now, and she hummed quietly to herself as she walked up the road to the train station. The last train of the day was waiting at the platform, so she hurried to get on, noticing as she did that a light in the CHRISTMAS LAND PARKING sign needed to be replaced, and making a mental note to tell Brendon, who had been voted the head of general maintenance.

The train rolled out of the station. By the time it stopped at Ings Forest, the light rain had turned to snow which was settling on the ground. A couple of inches threatened to soak Bonnie's shoes as she climbed off, although someone had been out to clear the road leading to Christmas Land.

As the train pulled away behind her, she followed the path through the forest, now brightly illuminated with fairy lights and Christmas displays. She smiled as a reindeer made from a frame of lights nodded its head, and a fairy-lit Father Christmas rose in and out of a chimney.

The park was visible through the trees long before she reached it, lights powered with batteries charged by solar panels in the chalet roofs creating a glittering display which would enchant any guest before they'd even stepped through the gates. She walked across freshly laid cobbles even as snowflakes landed and settled around her, past the waving Mr. Glockenspiel and three dancing elves.

Before heading back to the café, she ducked into the staff centre. Every business or member of staff had a postbox. Inside her own she flicked with amusement through a handful of circulars for Debbie, and a hard packet which was probably a delivered CD. She stuffed them into her bag to pass on, almost missing a letter at the bottom with a postmark from Swindon.

She froze. Fingers that had felt so sure of themselves now shook as she lifted it up. She didn't need to turn it over to check the return address, because she knew Steve's handwriting by heart. The scruffy, bunched nature of the letters, the way he had filled in some of the gaps like he had a bad case of OCD.

The temptation to open it immediately nearly overwhelmed her, but she stuffed it into her bag with the rest.

She would need to be sitting down when she opened it, she felt sure.

28

FAMILY BLUES

Barry's wedding was only part of a grand reopening fair over the first weekend of December. Aware that first impressions made the biggest impact, and that the park's second coming coincided with the internet revolution, they all knew that bad online reviews could be irreparably damaging. Therefore, over the last few days, everything was checked and double-checked, then checked all over again.

Bonnie stood in front of the café, holding up her phone. The wind rustled in the trees around her, showering her with clumps of recently accumulated snow. With a click she took a picture, then immediately began to scrutinize using the zoom. An ornament in the window looked a little out of place. She had forgotten to pull up a clump of weeds near the door. One of the sign's light bulbs was dimmer than the rest. She made a mental note of each issue then went to find Debbie.

They took a plate of marshmallows to a corner table. By the look of Debbie's fingers and the guilty grin on her face, she'd already tested the newest batch.

'I think we need to start up some kind of exercise regime,' Bonnie said. 'At this rate neither of us will be able to fit through the door by springtime.'

'I'd offer to climb the tree next time but I reckon I'd break it,' Debbie said. 'How about we go on a hike up to that lake later?'

Bonnie leaned forward. 'Did you just suggest going on a hike?'

Debbie scowled. 'Look, it's not just you who's gone all new age and new personality and all that since we showed up. Look at me. I'm wearing red socks.' Debbie stuck out a leg and jerked up her black jeans. 'I mean, that's just crazy.'

'They're very dark red,' Bonnie said, laughing. 'You could claim they were vampire red.'

'Cool. I need some way of explaining away this reindeer jumper too.' She leaned back and pulled open her coat to reveal a knitted reindeer with a flashing red nose.

'Ooh.' Bonnie grinned. 'How would you call it? Brutal.'

'You've got that right. I was hanging out down that bad taste shop yesterday, and Ben was in there. I kind of had to buy something to keep the conversation going.'

'Ben? Gene's grandson?'

'Yeah. He was in there, buying boots for his Father Christmas getup.'

'Are you sweet on him?'

Debbie laughed. '"Sweet on him"? Do you know what decade it is? I think we need to switch out the CD for some slightly less Christmas classics.'

'Don't avoid the question.'

Debbie scowled. 'It poses an interesting dilemma, that's for sure. I never expected to be in demand at a Christmas theme park.'

'In demand?'

'Shaun, he's like all "why don't we go to Download Festival together"?, and I'm like, bro, we've only just met.' Debbie sighed. 'And then there's Mitchell … I mean, what am I supposed to do? I sometimes wish it was you with the boyfriend issues so I could take a back seat.'

Bonnie laughed. 'I think I'm past all that.'

'Come on, Bon. You're only fifty-two. I mean, it seems like you're ancient to me, but to someone like Gene you'd be like Rapunzel or something.'

'My hair barely touches my shoulders.'

'I mean like, a princess. All independent young woman and all that.'

'I'm independent because I was forced to be, and I'd definitely swap out "young" for "getting older".'

'Ah, you're just modest. You're pretty. No one ever told you that?'

Bonnie frowned. The conversation was going into territory she didn't think she wanted to enter. Life with Phil hadn't always been bad. In the first few years she'd felt hopelessly in love, and thought that he felt the same. He had always complimented her, taken her out to dinner, bought her flowers … she couldn't clearly put her finger on when the shift had happened. It had been a gradual thing.

'I think we'd better get back to work,' she said. 'I need to do some weeding out the front, and I want you to cast your expert eye over the ornaments in the window. We have three days before the re-opening.'

Debbie rolled her eyes. 'Look at you, changing the subject. Well, according to Brendon, we're nearly fully booked this weekend, and there'll be a bunch more day visitors. Make sure you brush your hair, or wear some cute bonnet or something. Christmas romance and all that.'

'They'll all be kids or old men,' Bonnie said.

'Nothing wrong with a rich old man,' Debbie said. 'Didn't they used to call them patrons?'

'In the Middle Ages. I'm happy just concentrating on my job for now,' Bonnie said. 'And talking of which … let's get back to work.'

She left Debbie in charge of reordering the café's kitchen cupboards and headed outside. In a shed around the back she had found a couple of old gas heaters and a stack of outdoor chairs. One by one, she took them out, wiped them down, and carried them around the front. There were a few metal tables and some heavy-duty parasols hidden in the dark recesses at the back of the shed. The tables just needed a wipe down, but the parasols were covered in mould. Carrying them around the front, Bonnie fetched a bucket of soapy warm water and proceeded to scrub them down, one by one. Even wearing rubber gloves, her hands began to feel chapped, and the chilly wind was a constant companion, bringing the occasional flurry of snow blown from the trees to patter around her.

'Bonnie!'

The cry was faint, but one she recognised. She stood up, looking for Brendon's voice as the shout came again. Movement caught her eye and she turned around.

Through the trees, something moved. A blinking light rose through the screen of trees, rising into the air. At first she wasn't sure what it was, then she recognised the observation tower's lift, slowing rising through the central metal frame towards the open deck at the top.

The lift hadn't worked for twenty years, Brendon had said. While the tower remained open, it was a hard slog of several hundred metal steps up to the top. Now though, the whole thing pulsed with lights like a giant candy cane sticking up out of the forest. Brendon stood on the platform at the top, with Niall beside him. Together they both waved again as the lift came to a stop and a couple more people got out.

Bonnie waved back, a smile on her face. June, helping old Belinda out of the lift, came to stand beside Brendon, wrapping an arm around his shoulders. They looked so happy together, as a family. She held her smile for a few seconds longer, just in case they could see it over the distance, then went back to her cleaning, her head down, not wanting anyone to see her tears.

Steve's letter had been damning.

Mother,

Thanks I suppose for the ticket thing. I did take the time to look the place up on the internet, but it said it's abandoned? Have you gone and joined some cult or something? I have no idea what's going through your mind these days. I thought you were happy enough up in Weston but I guess idle minds and all that. I know I should have visited to keep an eye on you, but I'm busy with work and the family. Please don't do anything stupid. Did you really quit your job? Just don't come begging when you run out of money. You were doing all right before. There was no reason to take some drastic action. It'll be your own fault if you end up penniless.

I'm not sure if we'll be able to come or not. We're due to visit France with Dad and Cynthia in February half term so we'll play it by ear. We're not all made of money but thanks anyway for thinking of us.

I'll call you as soon as I have a chance.

Steve

Bonnie had read it twice and stuffed it into a drawer in

Mervin's desk, the words already seared into her heart. *I have no idea what's going through your mind. It'll be your own fault if you end up penniless. Don't come begging when you run out of money.*

She had bathed that little boy, held his hand to walk him to school, rolled around on the living room carpet and make aeroplane noises as he giggled and laughed. She had cooked every meal with love, taken him to endless parks, cheered him on at school football matches and taken him to every practice when he had joined a local team during his teenage years, a time when his father had been absent most of the time. Steve's memory of it was that his mother had been an embarrassment when all the other kids' dads were there, and that she should have got a better job so his dad could have worked less. Even as an adult, he was blind to everything that had happened, and perhaps the hardest line to read was that his family was visiting France with her ex-husband and that woman.

Thinking about the letter had sucked all the enthusiasm out of her. She emptied out her bucket and went to find Debbie.

'I'm tired,' she said. 'I need a break.'

'Sounds good. Where?'

'The pub.'

Debbie's grin told Bonnie all she needed to know. 'Say no more,' Debbie said.

~

A couple of hours later, Bonnie was leaning over her third or fourth glass of sherry, lamenting everything that was wrong about the world. Debbie, seemingly with the drinking capacity of a rugby prop forward, nodded sagely as Bonnie rambled, occasionally interjecting with words of encouragement.

'Like, if you son does show up, I'll wrap him up with Christmas lights, plug him into the wall and then hang him up by the balls from the ceiling. Not that I'm violent or anything, but he needs to learn respect. You're a wonderful person, Bon. Just because your son is too spoiled to see it, doesn't mean it's not true.'

'Claire never calls me either. I must have been such a terrible mother!'

'Rubbish. She never calls you because they probably don't have wifi on the moon. Give it another ten years and I'm pretty sure the Russians will have something going on.'

'I can't wait that long!'

'Bon, Bon, relax. Once they see how successful the café's going to be, they'll come around.'

'What's the use of anything if the park's going to close in January?'

'You really think that's going to happen? It just got a complete makeover. No one in their right mind would close it now.'

'How can you be sure?'

'Call it intuition. We'll be fine. Look, we have way more pressing concerns.'

'Like what?'

'The park opens in two days. We have to be bang on the money. And Barry's lot will show up. It's going to be utter chaos. I can't believe I got myself into this.' Debbie rubbed her forehead. 'I mean, what if Shaun, Ben, and Mitchell go at it in the middle of Barry's wedding? If Shaun and Ben are in costume, Father Christmas and an elf beating on a deaf guy, that's going to scar any children watching for life. *Scar* them, Bon.'

Bonnie wiped tears out of her eyes. 'It would make the greatest wedding video of all time.'

'Yeah, and destroy the childhoods of millions. You know Larry is a top YouTuber, right? He reviews video games. He has three million subscribers. That's influence, Bon. With thirty seconds of footage he could end Christmas forever, and it would be all my fault.'

Bonnie stared at the serious expression on Debbie's face as her friend downed the remaining half of her pint before wiping a sleeve across her mouth. Then, as if the whole world had turned on its head and stood there dangling precariously with its feet wiggling in the air, she burst into laughter.

29

GRAND REOPENING

'Okay, last minute checklist. We have regular milk, soy milk, almond milk, and coconut milk?'

Debbie nodded. 'Check.'

'And we have an ongoing order for more of the same every two days throughout December?'

'Uh … check.'

'We have chocolate, ground and in bars?'

'Check.'

'And we have cinnamon, nutmeg, Christmas spice, ginger, and turmeric?'

'Ah, yeah, I expect so.'

'Yes or no?'

'Let's go with yes?'

'I'll check for myself later. We're totally loaded with marshmallows?'

'You mean in the rack or in my stomach?'

Bonnie rolled her eyes. 'I suppose both. If you're full, you won't eat any more.'

Debbie spread her hands. 'What do you take me for? I

would never eat any of the stock. I stuffed myself in that new waffle place this morning while you were still getting dressed, just in case I got tempted.'

Bonnie smiled. 'Then we're all set. Let's go and meet the first arrivals.'

The official opening was at ten o'clock. With the first train arriving at Ings Forest station at nine thirty-five, everyone was hoping there would be a sizable crowd in attendance when Gene stepped up to cut the tape. The railway company had been persuaded to put on an extra carriage just in case. Overnight bookings were full, but with a strict limit of five hundred people per night, it would be the day customers who made the real difference.

'Do I really have to wear that outfit? I mean, come on, Bon, it's pink.'

'It's pink and white. It'll make you look nice, even with all those piercings and tattoos. You might even like it.'

'I will never, ever, ever like wearing pink.'

Bonnie lifted an eyebrow. 'I'm the boss.'

'Just for you, Bon. Just for you.'

~

Twenty minutes later, they joined the rest of the staff by the gates. Everyone was in full costume, but even so, Debbie and her bubblegum pink nineteen-fifties waitress outfit caught the most glances. Bonnie had found the costumes in a cupboard. Mervin had worn an orange and blue pinstripe suit, but Bonnie had decided to retire it in his honour. The old waiting staff uniforms would do until she could decide on some new designs, but if she were honest about it, they were no worse than what she had to wear at Morrico. With her hair done up in a bun, she actually felt quite stylish.

Christmas at the Marshmallow Cafe

'Here they come,' Brendon said. Gene, in full Victorian Father Christmas woodland garb, slammed him on the colourful back, causing a loud glockenspiel tune to play. June, frowning, reached across and adjusted a volume control.

Nearby, Shaun, Mark, and Alan were practicing some dance steps in freshly washed and ironed elf costumes. Jason had shown up with a reindeer, which snorted and pawed at the ground as he held it by the reins. Belinda wore traditional Lapland garb, and looked like an ancient tribal elder. Jan and Daniel from Bad Taste Christmas Goods wore matching jumpers with LED Christmas presents on the front, and from the look of some of the other catering staff, they had shared a few out. Only Niall, wearing a simple red Christmas hat with his bomber jacket and jeans, looked in any way normal.

The first customers appeared through the trees. Bonnie blinked at the size of the crowd; the train must have been packed. Those nearest the front appeared to be jogging to get there first. As the crowd assembled behind a ticker tape line, facing the staff across the plaza, Gene stepped forward, with Ben at his shoulder. Bonnie noticed how the big man limped a little, a grimace on his face hidden to anyone who didn't know him by his thick beard, like a warrior moving to his spot on the battlefield to make a last, valiant stand. With Ben beside him, dressed in similar but slightly less dramatic garb like a trainee actor learning from an old master, she sensed this was the moment the baton passed.

What had at first resembled a bedraggled old pine standing off to the side of the main square had been snipped and manicured into a magnificent Christmas tree nearly ten metres high, decked out in all manner of ornaments and lights. Gene, walking slowly as the crowd hushed, reached a podium and climbed up to a dais set up on the top. Ben stood respectfully on the step below, holding a thick extension cord leading from the tree in one hand, and a plug in the other.

'On this, the fifth of December,' Gene bellowed into a microphone, his voice echoing through the trees, 'I, Saint Nicholas of Myra in what is now known as Turkey, taker of all manner of names, Father Christmas, Santa Claus, Sinterklass, Chris Kringle, Ded Moroz, and a hundred others, declare, with the power of the North Pole, Greenland, and everywhere in between, that our magnificent Christmas Land, great bringer of magic to all who enter its gates, be returned, restored … reborn! Welcome, one and all, to the most magical place on this or any other earth. Welcome … to Christmas Land!'

He sagged as he hollered the last sentence, leaning on Ben's shoulder as his grandson struggled to hold him up. The crowd cheered. Bonnie noticed how Ben said something, but Gene gave a quick shake of the head, his hands reaching out as he regained his stance. Ben passed up the two wires, and Gene, his face contorting with pain, lifted the plug and socket above his head.

'We are … born again!'

As Gene connected the wires, the Christmas tree illuminated with a glow so bright that the nearest people covered their eyes. Flame-like lights flickered all over its branches, and a glittering star flickered red, blue and green. From somewhere behind came the tinkle of Christmas music, and then the gates began to move, a series of recently repaired cogs, wheels, and pistons rising and falling as bursts of steam rose out of little funnels and dissipated into the air.

As planned and practiced over the last few days, the staff quickly dispersed, some running to the ticket offices, others back into the park to take up their positions or start kettles boiling and ovens heating. Those in character dress made a guard of honour with Brendon dressed as Mr. Glockenspiel standing at the front, with Jason, still holding the reindeer, beside him. Gene, once again leaning on Ben's shoulder, stood alongside, waving as the first customers streamed towards the gates. Bonnie, standing off to the side with Debbie beside her, smiled at the sight of a few familiar faces. Larry and Mitchell gave her a wave, as did Barry, on the arm of a pretty young lady. She saw Tim and John, the elderly couple, shuffling forward, and there, behind them, to her surprise, was Jean, wearing a Christmas hat. 'The old goat gave me the weekend off!' Jean hollered in Bonnie's direction, frantically waving her hands over her head as the crowd took her forward. And a few steps behind her came Len from The King's Thistle, standing beside a tall, handsome young man who had to be his son, Thomas. Len noticed Bonnie and gave a polite wave which she returned with a wave and a smile.

'Is it over yet?' Debbie whispered beside her. 'Can I look up now?'

Bonnie started to laugh. 'I think you're okay,' she said. 'Come on, we'd better get in and get set up before they all get tired of the coaster and the sleigh rides.'

She was just about to head for the gates when she remembered Gene. As the crowd made their way through the ticket turnstiles, she saw him, standing behind, supported by Ben, still waving at the last customers as they filed inside. Brendon, his duties over, turned towards him, getting there just a step before Bonnie and Debbie.

'Are you all right?' he asked.

Gene winced. 'Think I might need a little more than Christmas magic for this one,' he muttered. 'Anyone got a phone that works?'

Debbie pulled out her smartphone. 'Picked myself up a roving wifi hotspot,' she said, pulling up emergency services and giving the button a quick tap. 'Songs were taking far too long to download. Now, where's the best way in for an ambulance?'

30

WEDDINGS AND POSSIBILITIES

'Now, Barnard Jonas Winkleton, please repeat after me. "I do take thee, Catherine Savoy Lane-Jenkins, to be my lawful wedded wife."'

As Barry repeated the vicar's words, Debbie, standing in the fourth row beside Bonnie, sniggered.

'Why do rich people always have the stupidest names?' she whispered.

'Shh! Have you been on the punch already?'

'No, but come on, Winkleton? Savoy? What kind of a middle name is that? Was she named after the hotel where she was conceived or something?'

'Better than Number 9 Bus Shelter,' Bonnie whispered back. 'I remember your mother telling me that was her second choice for your middle name after Maud, but your dad and the postman outvoted her two to one.'

'Shut up. How did you know my middle name was Maud?'

'After you left your wallet at the pub the other night, I had a quick glance through to make sure nothing had been stolen. Look, here they come. Get ready to throw that confetti.'

'Good call on shredding last year's menus,' Debbie said, holding up a bag of colourful paper.

'Out with the old, in with the new,' Bonnie said. 'I felt it was best to put my own mark on things.'

'Judging by the crowd yesterday, it's going all right.'

Bonnie smiled. Her arms still ached from a long evening of preparing marshmallows, after completely selling out during the first day. She'd sold more in five hours of business than she'd expected to sell in the first week. Several return customers had spoken of their love for Mervin's café, and told her how glad they were that the place was open again. Bonnie was of course delighted, but aware she would need to hire more staff if she wanted to have any energy left by Christmas.

A clanging of bells signaled the end of the ceremony. Bonnie and Debbie joined the other guests as they filed out, heading for the plaza outside of the wedding chapel where photographs would be taken. As they stood around in the cold while flakes of snow fell around them, delighting the main party guests, Bonnie eyed the restaurant forum across the plaza.

'Do you think they'd notice if we headed over to the reception a little early?' she said.

Debbie shrugged. 'I imagine they could grab a picture off the website and Photoshop you into the group pic if they really wanted to. Let's go.'

An area of the restaurant forum was cordoned off for the wedding reception, but the rest was open for regular customers. Bonnie and Debbie ordered a couple of coffees and took them to a terrace which overlooked the group milling around in the plaza outside. A photographer the wedding party had brought with them was attempting to organise people into groups, while another from Christmas Land, a man dressed in a brightly coloured ragdoll outfit, was also attempting to take pictures, cajoling small groups to make cartoonish expressions for his bubblegum coloured, oversized camera.

'Is that Mark in there?' Bonnie asked.

Debbie shook her head. 'Alan.'

'How can you tell?'

'I saw him pinch a glass of sparkling off the buffet table just before the ceremony started. And he mentioned it in the pub yesterday. Said he'd be breaking out a new costume today and he was a bit nervous.'

'I'm not surprised. He's doing a good job, though.'

A shadow fell over the table. Bonnie looked up to see Len standing there, with Thomas beside him.

'Bonnie, there you are. I went over to the café but the lad you left in charge said you'd be here.'

'Thanks for coming back again, Len.'

Len smiled. 'We had such a great time yesterday that we couldn't resist coming again today, could we, Thomas? Plus, I don't have my lad home so often.'

Thomas smiled. 'Dad always said this place was tacky. I have no idea what he was talking about.'

'Amazing what a bit of paint can do,' Bonnie said.

'You should be so proud,' Len said. 'It's fantastic. And there are so many people here. You know, my guest rooms were full yesterday because there weren't enough chalets available onsite.'

'We have a strict limit,' Bonnie said. 'Part of the environmental agency contract, apparently.'

'And I had to bust out the karaoke machine for a group on their way home last night too,' Len continued. 'I've never heard Christmas songs sung so loud.'

Bonnie became aware of Debbie kicking her under the

table. She ignored it as long as possible before giving Debbie a sharp glare. Debbie mouthed something and rolled her eyes.

'Anyway, I was hoping to catch up with you because I remember you were asking about a book,' Len said. 'I went round to see my old dad a couple of days ago and he had a copy. I couldn't bring it up to the park because I gather it's a bit of a collectors' item, but it looked complete. If you could stop by the pub in the next few days I'll gladly let you have a look.'

Bonnie could barely bring herself to speak. She stared at Len, aware Debbie was assaulting her leg again like a frustrated kickboxer.

'Sure,' she said. 'I certainly could. I'll be busy over the next couple of days until the wedding party has gone back, but I'll definitely have time over the weekend.'

The spotlights set into the room appeared to have given Len's cheeks a reddish tint. 'Sounds good,' he said. 'I look forward to seeing you.'

As Len and Thomas headed off in the direction of the reindeer enclosure, Debbie gave Bonnie's leg one more swift kick.

'Good god, will you stop that?'

Debbie leaned forward. 'I was trying to get your attention.'

'Attention got. Why?'

Debbie held up three fingers. 'Which one was missing?'

'Do I need to find a pair of scissors or something?'

'His wife! Where's his wife?'

Bonnie shrugged. 'Perhaps she was shopping or something? I mean, some of the shops here sell some pretty nice stuff.'

Debbie shook her head. 'No. Are you really not seeing this?'

'Seeing what?'

'You're what, fifty-five?'

'You know I'm fifty-two! My birthday's not even until September.'

'And Len, he's about the same, right? His son—his really handsome son—is at the tail end of a university degree, so he's what, twenty-two, twenty-three? If Len had kids around thirty, he'd be what, fifty-three, fifty-four?'

'I'm pretty sure we're not going to need a calculator to figure all this out.'

'Tell me, have you ever seen his wife?'

Bonnie frowned. She had visited the pub a few times, but seen no sign of any woman in Len's life. She had mentioned bringing his wife and son to the park, but Len had neither confirmed nor denied the existence of a woman in his life. And there was something about him that was attractive, something difficult to place at first. On the surface he was plain-looking, mostly bald, wide-shouldered but soft around the face, his features subdued rather than prominent. But he was kind, and when he talked to her she could tell he really listened. He wasn't just waiting for his turn to speak.

'Please don't suggest you're thinking to match-make me.'

Debbie grinned. 'Oh, Bon. Would I ever do such a thing?'

31

INVESTIGATIONS

The wedding reception was a riotous affair which went on until nearly midnight. Bonnie, feeling her years, ducked out long before Debbie did, later hearing her friend stumbling up the stairs some time in the small hours. Aware that customers waited for no one, Bonnie pulled herself out of bed just after six o'clock and made her way to the kitchen to get herself some coffee.

It was set to be another busy day. While it was only December 7th, with several weeks yet before Christmas, she hadn't felt so festive in years. In Morrico, relentless lines of shoppers humming along to the day's fifteenth play of Slade tended to squeeze out any excitement. Now, despite a mild hangover, she found herself humming the very same Christmas tune she had come to loathe over her supermarket years, as she made coffee and carried it upstairs, through the grotto and onto the rooftop terrace.

Christmas Land was beginning to wake up. Snow had fallen overnight, but the parasol Bonnie had set up over her little table and chair had kept them clear. She sat down, listening to the birds singing in the trees, her thick dressing gown keeping out most of the morning chill. Like a giant dragon, the coaster made a lethargic trail through the trees, its first empty run of the day always a slow loop to make sure the tracks were clear of branches or accumulated snow.

Even at this time of the morning, she heard the laughter of children, already outside playing in the snow, and the frustrated cries of sleepy parents telling them to put on hats and gloves or zip up their jackets. Bonnie smiled, taking a deep breath as she sipped her coffee. It was set to be a good day. A phone call last night from Ben had told her that Gene was stable in hospital, and might even be out by Christmas, although he would be in strict rocking chair duties. And later in the evening, she had bumped into Jean, enthusiastically displaying a sparkling new Christmas jumper. Although Jean had clearly been on the sherry, she had sounded pretty interested in a potential assistant manager position, should one become available.

There was only the problem of the letter. Bonnie shifted uncomfortably. Len claimed to have found a copy of the book, but after Debbie's assertions, the thought of visiting him made her feel awkward. She hadn't come here for this, but now that the seed was planted … he did have a nice smile, she had to admit.

She finished her coffee and headed downstairs. Snoring came from Debbie's room, so Bonnie tiptoed past to the shower, got herself ready and then headed downstairs to prepare the café for opening.

In the face of unexpected demand, June had lent Bonnie Niall's services, but after leaving the boy in charge during the wedding reception, Bonnie was feeling guilty about asking him to work more hours, particularly when June was also busy over in the Mountain Breeze. Perhaps it was time to send Jean an official job offer. If only she had an assurance that the park would stay open past January. Everything was rosy now, but what if it fell away after Christmas? The threat of the mysterious letter hung heavy over her head.

The café opened every day at ten, but since Bonnie was ready by nine, she decided to take a walk over to the staff building and check her postbox. Outside, the fresh snow on the ground reminded her she needed to buy herself some proper snow boots, because her Wellingtons didn't do a great job of keeping her feet warm. Having never experienced such snowfall down on the Weston-super-Mare seafront, she hadn't realised how totally unprepared she was for a real winter until she came here.

Halfway there, she bumped into Jason, pushing a wheelbarrow of dry feed towards the reindeer enclosure.

'A fine morning it is,' he greeted her. 'How was the wedding yesterday?'

'Fantastic,' she said. 'I'm exhausted, though. I'm getting a little old for parties.'

'Brendon was telling me how we've already had a couple more requests come in,' he said. 'People were posting pictures online even before yesterday's wedding had finished. News travels fast these days.'

'I suppose it is a unique experience,' Bonnie said. 'Getting married in a Christmas theme park.'

'Brendon suggested that we offer romantic wedding sleigh rides as part of the package. Honestly, we're going to have a lot of thinking to do if the park stays open.'

'If it stays open.' Bonnie nodded. 'What would you do if it doesn't?'

Jason shrugged. 'I have a degree in zoology and conservation management, so I guess I'd try to find work in a zoo or safari park somewhere. I'd worry about the deer, though. We couldn't just set them loose, and the idea of culling them ... I can't think about it. They're like friends to me.'

'I'm sure the park won't close,' Bonnie said, trying to sound confident. 'Not after all the work we've done to get it up and running properly again.'

'You're right,' Jason said, but his eyes betrayed his thoughts. 'Those letters were just a warning. I don't think we have anything to worry about.'

They went their separate ways, Jason heading for the reindeer enclosure, Bonnie for the staff building near the entrance. Brendon, Mark, Shaun, and Alan were clearing snow from the courtyard plaza outside the main gates. Bonnie stopped to watch the bizarre sight of a court jester and three elves working away with snow shovels. When they noticed her, she smiled and waved. Brendon thumped his back to produce a brief jingle, and the three elves did a quick dance step, finishing with a flourishing bow.

Inside the staff building, she found several other members of support and maintenance staff setting up for the day or working on computers. She put her head round the door of the office and gave the people inside a wave, then invited them over for free hot chocolate and marshmallows as soon as they had a break.

She had redirected her mail from her Weston address, and found several Christmas cards stuffed inside. Three were circulars: one from her local hair salon, one from the mechanic who usually did a shoddy job of looking after her car, and one from an online company she had used just once six years ago to buy a four-slice toaster, and now insisted on reminding her that she was a valued customer year after year after year.

There were also a couple of personal ones too, from an old neighbour who had moved to London, and from a cousin who lived in Stockport whom Bonnie hadn't seen in twenty years, but who kept her in the loop with a colourful two-sheet family newsletter about people Bonnie had never met. She smiled, appreciating the effort, but wishing they'd use the printer ink for something more beneficial. Still, the card had a pretty robin design and she had already planned to hang them up around the café with some old ones of Uncle Mervin's she had found in a store cupboard.

Below them, she found an unpaid gas bill, and a reminder that her car insurance would be due in February. Then, at the very bottom, she found a letter.

The stamp and postmark were from Bulgaria. The handwriting—her address in Weston, but with a redirection sticker over the top—also familiar. Almost too long ago to remember, she had seen the first shapes of those letters as she held the hand steady, helping her five-year-old daughter to write her weekend diary for school.

Her hands shook as she tore the seal and pulled out the piece of paper.

Mother, greetings! Just a short note to let you know that I might be able to make it after all. Was planning to stay in Sofia over Christmas and New Year but I'm getting a bit homesick for the taste of good old mince pies. Can't guarantee it but I'll do my best. My laptop fell in a river (don't ask!) and I ended up losing your new address, so if you could pop a note in the post to the address below, I'd be eternally grateful. Fingers crossed, eh. Bye!x

At the bottom of the note was the address for a post office in Sofia. So excited she could barely think straight, Bonnie borrowed some notepaper and an envelope from the staff office and hastily scribbled down a note for her daughter. Claire had promised before and never shown up—once even claiming to have spent Christmas on a bus in Switzerland having been trapped in heavy snow for three days—but Bonnie never failed to get excited at the prospect.

With the letter sealed and the address written, Bonnie fussed around, trying to find a stamp. No one in the office had one, but someone reminded her of the Christmas Land Post Office, in a little log cabin next to the restaurant forum, where she could buy stamps with an official Christmas Land logo.

There wasn't much time left before the café had to open, so Bonnie headed back to check on Debbie. To her surprise, Debbie was already up and about, and in uniform, no less. She gave Bonnie a wide grin as she came through the door.

'Surprised?' she said. 'I heard you go out. Figured you'd get sidetracked somewhere and leave me to do all the work. I cleaned out the coffee machine filter and made a decent brew with the dregs. You game?'

Bonnie winced. 'I'll pass. Thanks for everything. I've just got to nip up to the post office for a moment.'

'Oh? Something happen?'

Bonnie told her about the letter from Claire.

'That's great. Reckon she'll actually show up? I don't mean to dump on your parade, but didn't she promise to come back last Christmas?'

'She got caught in an airline strike in France.'

'Yeah, that. And the Christmas before?'

'That was the bus incident.'

Debbie sighed. 'You're the best mother in the word, Bon. Well, second best after mine. I always knew she was awesome from when she gave me a Maiden CD for my eleventh birthday. None of this whole, "Sweetheart, can't you listen to Backstreet Boys instead?" rubbish. It was like, "don't keep shoplifting metal CDs from that shop at the end of the street, because you know his bottom line is tight. I'll just buy them for you instead." But you get what I mean. Your kids are punks.'

'Um, thanks.'

'Seriously. I mean, I hope I'm wrong, but you don't deserve to be treated like a doormat. You've done so much for so many people. Look, I've got today. You go and take a break, go into Quim and do some shopping or something. Get your nails done.'

'Do they have manicurists in Quim?'

Debbie shrugged. 'No idea. Go and have a look. Post your letter while you're at it, but have some you time. Seriously.'

'You're going to be busy.'

Debbie shrugged. 'Larry said he'd help out.'

'Larry?'

Debbie frowned. 'What? He's cool. Yeah, I know he looks like a potato wrapped in a Burberry blanket but he's sharp as a whistle. Needs to sort out his music tastes, but you can't have everything. And he's an influencer.'

'A what?'

'He posts a video online saying jump and a whole lot of people do it. That's the new power structure, Bon.'

'Great.'

'So, I'm thinking to set you up an online marshmallow shop.'

Bonnie winced. 'There's only so much marshmallow these hands can make.'

'We'll get staff.'

'In that case, I think I'll leave you in charge of recruiting.'

'My pleasure. I'd make sure they all had perfect music tastes and no weird habits.' Debbie picked up a broom and swished it in Bonnie's direction. 'Right, you. Out. It's your day off.'

Bonnie smiled. 'Thanks.'

~

Despite Debbie's misgivings about Claire's sincerity, Bonnie headed to the post office, bought a stamp with a little picture of Father Christmas leaning over the Christmas Land logo, and dropped the letter into the postbox. Afterwards, she took a walk around the park, stopping to talk to some of the people she had become friendly with such as Belinda, and Jan from the Bad Taste Christmas Goods shop. On her way, she stopped by Gene's place to see if Ben had any news.

'He says he's fine,' Ben laughed. 'The old fool. He tried to get out of bed and nearly fell on his face. They told him to start following the rules, and he bellowed that he was Father Christmas and that magic would take him home.'

'I wish it would.'

'Me too. Unfortunately he's going to have to rely on more conventional medicine.'

'Do you still think he'll be home by Christmas?'

'I don't think he'd have it any other way. He's been Father Christmas here every year since the park opened. He wants me to take over, but he doesn't want me to at the same time, you know what I mean?'

'He can't let go of the past.'

'Something like that. Where are you off today?'

Bonnie told him about her forced day off. 'Debbie thinks I'm working too hard, so I've been sent for some retail therapy.'

'It's easy to throw yourself into it, isn't it?' Ben said. 'When you see the smiles of the kids, hear the laughter …

beats working in a bank. That's what I was doing before. Becoming a trainee Father Christmas wasn't quite the career change I was looking for, but now that I'm here … I can't think of anywhere else I'd rather be. It really is quite lovely.'

Bonnie smiled. 'I know.'

~

The station at Quimbeck was bustling with people ready to make their way up to Christmas Land. Bonnie pushed through the throng, silently wishing Debbie good luck as she caught a couple of snippets of conversation praising her marshmallows. It was set to be a busy day.

Quim was relatively quiet, with a few older people wandering up and down its narrow streets, taking pictures, going in and out of the pretty shops or sitting on benches that surrounded its quaint square, eating cakes or lumps of fudge out of paper bags.

Above, a grey sky hung heavy with the threat of more snow. Bonnie's breath steamed as she wandered about, with no interest in shopping or getting any kind of makeover, trying to delay the inevitable.

Finally, she could no longer put it off any more, so she headed for The King's Thistle. The pub wasn't yet open, but Len was setting up tables and chairs beneath parasols on the wide patio area. Bonnie climbed a set of steps to the fence surrounding the beer garden and waited until he noticed her.

'Bonnie! How nice to see you.'

Was there a hint of a blush in his cheeks, or was it just from the exertion of carrying out the tables and chairs? Bonnie felt like a shy schoolgirl, her heart thundering, words that had come so easily before Debbie's observation now stumbling on her tongue like drunks leaving a Christmas party.

'Hey Len, I, uh, just stopped by to ask if now was a good time to, um, take a look at the book you found.'

'Sure. Come on in. With this weather I'm not expecting a lot of people this morning.'

He headed into the pub, leaving Bonnie to trail behind. He held the door for her, then offered her coffee, which she agreed to with a silent nod.

'Thomas and I had a great time at the park,' he said. 'We'll certainly visit again before the Christmas season is over. He's gone into Kendal today, and I couldn't leave Mal in charge of the pub yet again.'

'Mal? Your wife?' Bonnie blurted.

Len laughed. 'Malcolm. My second-in-command. He needs a day or two off sometimes. We're pretty flat out at this time of year.'

'Oh. Right.'

'Come on back. We're not open yet.'

He disappeared through a bead curtain. Bonnie stood dumbly by the entrance for a few seconds until Len reappeared.

'Come on, don't be shy.'

Trying not to show any obvious signs of discomfort, Bonnie followed him behind the bar and through the curtain. She found herself in a narrow connecting corridor with another open door a few steps in front. This led through into a small but comfortable living room. All stone walls and white-washed ceiling beams, it had an open fire flickering behind a fire guard, and lines of bookshelves fitted into the irregular walls at haphazard angles, the kind of DIY project that must have taken weeks and no little skill. On a mantel over the fire, several pictures displayed a happy family of three, Len, Thomas, and a homely, attractive lady Bonnie assumed had to be Len's wife. In one, a much younger Len was smiling while his wife held a baby. In another, a tall, handsome boy beamed as he held up a certificate, with older versions of each parent standing beside him. In another, the woman, this time wearing a headscarf, hugged Thomas, now in his late teens, as they both smiled at the camera.

Something in Bonnie's stomach knotted. This felt like a private place, one where she was an intruder. She wanted to be gone as soon as possible.

'Here,' Len said, carrying in a book from another room and setting it down on the table. 'This is it, isn't it?'

Bonnie, happy to be distracted from the memories steeped into the living room's walls, peered at the cover. 'It looks like it,' she said.

'Do you remember what page you needed to see?'

'Yes. Is it okay for me to touch?'

Len smiled. 'Sure.'

Bonnie flicked over the pages, turning each gently. The book had a similar feel to the other, barely looked at, a historical document to be kept rather than something to be read over time and time again. One page before the one she wanted, she paused, afraid to turn it over. What kind of mystery would she reveal, if any?

'Go on, then,' Len said, giving her a gentle pat on the shoulder. 'Don't be afraid.'

Bonnie took a deep breath, and turned over the page.

32

MYSTERIES UNEARTHED

At first she wasn't sure what she was looking at. The black and white photograph had not transferred to the book very well, leaving faces grainy. Five men stood in a semi-circle, staring at the picture. She recognised the man on the right as Gene, his beard shorter than now, revealing a powerful, youthful face. Beside him was a man labeled as Donald Connelly. Taller even than Gene, he was more slender, clean shaven, with piercing eyes that stared straight at the camera. Bonnie glanced up at Len, and saw a younger version looking back.

'My father,' he said. 'He didn't last long up there, so I heard. He sold his share and bought this pub. Told me he got claustrophobic among so many trees.'

On the other side of the semi-circle were a man and a woman. The man was Mervin, and Bonnie stared for a long time at the face which had given her everything, a face she barely knew. He wore a cheeky grin as though his life was one long joke, and had his arm around the person on the outside of the semi-circle, the only woman.

Belinda Chadfield.

It was the same Belinda, surely. The elderly woman Bonnie had slowly begun to befriend was one of the park's founders. In her youth she had been strikingly attractive, hair falling over her shoulders and curving in below her neck. She looked like a fashion model, even from the way she had angled her body to allow the camera to catch her from the side. Considering the rest of the people in the picture, she looked a little out of place.

'That doesn't help, does it?' Len said. 'I mean, it's something of a joke, isn't it?'

'I don't know,' Bonnie said, staring at the fifth and final member of the group.

In full Father Christmas garb, the man standing in the middle was labeled simply Saint Nick. His identity was hidden behind the beard and beneath the Christmas hat he wore. In the black and white photographs the colours he wore were uncertain, but from the shadows Bonnie guessed they were shades of dark green, perhaps even the same or a similar coat to the one Gene wore.

'Saint Nick,' she said. 'The letters were signed S.N. Saint Nick. Are we being pranked?'

'I suppose it depends who that man is,' Len said. 'I can ask my father, if you like. He's losing his marbles a bit, but he might remember.'

'I would really appreciate it.'

'Why don't you relax for a while? I'll make a phone call.'

He disappeared into another room, leaving Bonnie alone. She stared at the photograph for a couple of minutes before the weight of history began to bear down on her, making her feel small, a footnote on the reel of Christmas Land's long history. Instead, she got up and wandered across to the nearest bookshelf, reading the spines of the books. It appeared Len was an avid science fiction reader, with a collection of classic novels standing alongside several books on geology and geography. Near the end of one shelf, however, she came to a section of self-help books grouped together. *Switching the Lights On: Stepping Back into the World. Dealing with Grief in Ten Easy Steps. Turning your Pain into Gain. Living through Grief: A Practical Guide.*

'Bonnie?'

She spun around. Len stood in the doorway, a mobile phone in one hand. He smiled and cocked his head.

Bonnie felt her cheeks redden. 'Sorry, I was just looking around.'

Len shrugged. 'That's okay. Listen, I spoke to my father. I'm afraid he couldn't help. He's not in great health, and although he remembered the park, he couldn't recall the day of that photograph, nor who might have been wearing the costume.'

'It's okay,' Bonnie said. 'I'll ask Belinda when I go back. She might remember.'

'Sure.'

Len watched her. Aware she was still standing next to the self-help books, Bonnie found words moving into her mouth to fill the empty space, tumbling over her tongue.

'Your wife … she passed away, didn't she?'

Len's brow furrowed and he looked down at his feet with an expression of such sorrow Bonnie wanted to run across the room and pull him into her arms. He looked as though the rods that had held him upright had abruptly dissolved, leaving him frameless, immobile. Bonnie watched as he composed himself, taking a moment to rub his eyes before looking up once more.

'Two years ago,' he said. 'Bone marrow cancer. We couldn't find a donor in time.'

'I'm so sorry.'

'Don't be. I've come through the worst of it. There are

still dark days, but most of them are bright enough. Working in a pub helps, believe it or not. Just being around people, sharing conversation, it makes such a difference. And Thomas, he was a rock. She fell ill during his A-Levels but somehow still got the grades to get onto a dentistry course. Amanda—that was my wife's name—pushed him every step of the way. I was wallowing in despair, but she wouldn't let anyone get down. She wanted to see him pass, and he did.' Len pointed at the picture with the certificate. 'That was a document confirming his place. This one, with the headscarf, was taken the day he left for university. She wouldn't let him miss the start of his course, but she died during the Christmas holidays that first year. One reason I find it hard to get excited about the festive season.'

'I can understand. It must have been terrible for you.'

'She was a good woman, my wife. One of the best. But what's done is done, isn't it?'

Bonnie thought of her own life, how what she considered the tragedies were still open-ended, capable of being repaired. Her daughter might come home, her son might come around. To have something happen that was so final, a delete button pressed on a section of your life … it was hard just to think about.

'Do you want another drink?' Len said, nodding at her empty coffee cup. 'The pub doesn't open for another half an hour. I promise not to bore you with tales of misery.'

Bonnie smiled. 'Sure,' she said. 'I know they wouldn't be boring. Tell away.'

※

Half an hour turned into an hour, only interrupted when a couple of regulars banged on the pub's front door, asking to be let in. Bonnie was disappointed their conversation had to end, because it had been anything but boring or miserable. Len turned out to be a fine storyteller, filled with interesting information about the Lake District and its surrounds, a keen student of its myths and legends. She could have sat and listened to his stories all day, even finding it frustrating when he frequently paused and attempted to change the subject to her own life, as thought worried he was hogging their communal airtime. The truth was, Bonnie couldn't think of much to say except for sharing a couple of anecdotes about her old job that would shock shoppers if they knew. Len laughed, sounding interested. Bonnie tried to recall Debbie's encouragement and throw off the shackles of low confidence; unfortunately it was easier said than done.

On her way back, all the doubts began to return. It didn't matter than Len had sounded sincere when telling her to come back and let him know what happened at the end of her mysterious treasure hunt; she felt sure he was only saying that, trying to be nice. He seemed like a good guy, so why would he be interested in her? Whatever attractiveness she might once have had she had left behind on the bus of her early twenties. And who could compete against a ghost?

Every table on the patio outside the café was full. Bonnie smiled as she watched two children making a snowman while their parents watched from a table nearby. The woman, young and attractive, wore a baby harness, with the face of a sleeping baby, no more than a couple of months old, peering out of the top.

'Alan,' she said to the man seated opposite, could you go and ask if they have any formula milk? I left ours back at the chalet.' As the man stood up, the woman patted the baby harness, then turned to the children. 'John, Lily, don't let your drinks get cold.'

Bonnie made a mental note to order a couple of boxes of baby formula. There was some, but she would likely need more for the Christmas holiday season which was only a couple of weeks away. It would be a nice gesture to offer it for free to young mothers. While her children might be grown, she remembered how hard it had been when they were young. Wonderful, of course, but at times backbreaking.

Through the window she caught sight of Debbie and Larry behind the counter. Both were laughing and smiling despite the rush of customers. Confident that the café was in good hands, she headed for Belinda's clothing shop.

The old woman looked up as she entered. The shop, at the far end of the park, was empty. Belinda sat behind the counter reading a book on wild flowers. Bonnie paused, breathing in the scent of lavender over the top of the mustiness of leather. She glanced around at the racks of traditional dress, some for sale, others for hire, and wondered what kind of costume Belinda had worn all these years.

'Hello, dear,' Belinda said, noticing Bonnie for the first time. With slow, arthritic fingers, she closed the book and placed it gently down on the counter top. 'To what do I owe this pleasure? Not looking for an alternative uniform for your café, are you?'

Bonnie shook her head. 'I wanted to ask you something,' she said.

'Oh?'

Bonnie pulled out her phone and found a picture she had taken of the group in the book. She held it up for Belinda to see. The old woman leaned forward, lifted her glasses, and squinted.

'Well I never,' she said. 'How the years pass. I was quite a looker back then, wasn't I?'

'Do you remember when that was taken?'

Belinda chuckled. 'Oh, the memories. Of course I do. I might have lost the looks, but I've still got the brains.'

'The label says that this is the group who founded the park.'

'Yes, that's right. It is. There's Don and Gene, Merv—quite the charmer he was back then, although we fizzled out after a couple of years, sad to say—me, over there, and Nick, in his getup as always.'

'Nick?'

'You don't recognise him?'

'Should I?'

'I'd have thought, perhaps. That beard was natural, you know. He'd stick pine needles into it, for effect, he always said.'

'I have no idea who that is.'

'Oh, shame and circumstances. I'm surprised by that, I really am. That's Nicholas Green.' Belinda paused as though to allow the information to sink in. 'He was our financier, putting up the initial cash for the park to be built. Your grandfather.'

Bonnie felt her knees weaken. She reached out for the countertop. Belinda lifted a wispy eyebrow.

'Are you all right, dear? Would like a chair? There's one in the corner over there.'

'I'll be fine,' Bonnie said. 'I'm just a little shocked. My dad used to tell me stories about Christmas Land, but he never said it was owned by my family. I don't get it. I got nothing when my father died. What little there was went to my mother.'

'You don't know your grandfather?'

'My grandparents on my mother's side were always around. It felt at the time as though I only had one set, that the others were absent because there was no space for them. I don't remember ever really talking about it. I heard my father mention once about his mother's passing, but there was never any mention of his father. As though he didn't exist. After my dad died when I was twelve, everything shifted to my mother's side of the family. My father's side became a footnote.'

'That's a shame, but isn't it true that the practical doesn't often mix well with the mystical?'

Bonnie frowned. 'I'm not sure I understand.'

'Your grandfather, Nicholas, he was such a wonderful man. But at the same time he was very elusive and mysterious. I met him at university, don't you know. He was a lecturer. All of us were there at the same time, me, Gene, Mervin and Donald. Nicholas taught a course called Symbolism and Festival studies. We loved him. So full of life. He had this massive beard which reduced him to a pair of eyes, and he always wore the most wonderful clothes. I looked forward to his classes every week. Then, one day, he called the four of us aside.'

'What happened?'

'He told us he had come into some money and some land, and that he wanted to build a theme park. He needed some young, enthusiastic people to run it. He said he had chosen us based on our answers in a recent assignment based on Christmas mythology.'

'How strange that must have been.'

'Indeed it was. We were young, full of excitement for the world, but even so, it was a big decision. Merv, as he was Nicholas's son, was already roped in, but the rest of us had to be convinced. Gene and myself were an easy sell, but Donald less so. Eventually we all got talked around. And so Christmas Land came about. We finished our studies, moved up here, and oversaw the building and the opening of the theme park. Nicholas offered us a ten percent stake each. Donald didn't last long, selling his stake to Brendon's father and moving down to Quim, where he opened the pub they have there. He didn't like all the trees, preferred the fells and the meres. The rest of us, though, we loved every minute of it.'

'So what happened to my grandfather?'

Belinda smiled. 'Well, here's the thing. He wasn't around for long. He spent a few weeks teaching Gene how to do a good Father Christmas, then he departed, leaving us in charge. He went full silent partner, signing over the running to those of us who remained. I assumed he'd returned to his teaching position, but as the years passed, I thought of him less and less.'

'So, if he owned sixty percent of the park, why didn't he leave that to Mervin or my father? All I got was Mervin's lease, something I'm not allowed to sell.'

Belinda's eyes twinkled, taking years off her. 'Have you ever considered that your grandfather might still be alive?'

Bonnie stared. 'He couldn't be, could he? He'd be ancient by now. I mean, I'm fifty-two—'

'It's possible. He was in his forties when I knew him. He'd be close to the big one hundred, but he might just be holding on.'

'But where is he?'

Belinda smiled. 'I couldn't tell you that, dear,' she said. 'I think you might need to just trust your intuition.'

'That doesn't help.'

'I know.' Belinda sighed. 'I'm an old lady now. There won't be many more Christmases left in me, but those few that I have got, I want to enjoy. Would you like a hot chocolate? With extra cream?'

Bonnie laughed. 'I'd love one.'

33

TRUSTING FATE

Dark had fallen and a light snow was pattering on the ground. The café had closed at six o'clock, but Bonnie was sitting outside, relaxing with a hot chocolate left over from the day's makings. Her arms ached and her back needed a good rub, but otherwise she felt fantastic, her body filled with a warm glow. Her supermarket job had been a dull grind, swiping items and cards, handing over bags and change to people whose expressions told her they'd rather be anywhere else. And that was on the good days. Being lambasted for mistakenly swiping something twice, or blamed because the shop was out of a certain type of biscuit or brand of teabag … it had become part of the grind, something she had dully accepted as part of her lot.

But now … feeling the buzz of excitement as people pushed through the door fresh from a ride on the coaster or an ascent of the viewing tower, bags of toys in hands, talking with thrilled tones about how the park's Father Christmas had been out shoveling snow, only to stop and pull a handful of presents out of his jacket … then marvelling at the exotic marshmallows and variations of hot chocolate on the menu, gasping with delight as Bonnie handed across a foaming monstrosity of bubblegum bright colours … it never got old. She felt as though for the first time in her life she was doing something worthwhile.

Then there was the conversation. No one was angry or frustrated, tired of their job or annoyed with the kids, everyone had something positive to say. She began to recognise familiar faces, those staying for a week or more who visited daily, older groups, young couples, families with children. She learned names, home cities, jobs, favourite subjects at school, and when many told her they would certainly return she found herself already looking forward to it. Some, like the boys from Bristol or the elderly male couple, were already on their second visit. John and Tim were coming over for dinner tomorrow night, and Bonnie was looking forward to getting to know the two smiling old men, as well as hearing tales of this other wonderful Christmas village they had told her they visited every season. Life, for the first time in years, felt like life; she was alive, creating positive waves, doing something beyond just helping others to tick the boxes of their own uninspired existence.

Across the plaza, she watched Debbie comically bend to kiss the much shorter Larry on the cheek, before stopping to watch him wander away into the dark, in a direction which could lead either to the chalets or the restaurant forum and the pub. It looked like Debbie had finally made a choice from her many suitors, deciding on Larry, who had decided to stay until the spring at least, maintaining his social media empire from his chalet while working part time in both the café and one of the forum's restaurants.

After Larry had vanished into the dark, Debbie turned

and made her way over to the table. Bonnie took a couple of glasses off a tray and lifted a bottle of wine.

'Ready for a nightcap?' she asked.

'What's the poison?'

'Sauvignon from Chile. A customer gave it to me today, said it was to thank me for the great drinks over the last few days.' Bonnie smiled. 'I know he bought it in the grocery shop next to June's, but I appreciate the thought.'

'Don't mind if I do,' Debbie said. 'Been a hell of a day.'

'Are you and Larry an item now?'

Debbie shrugged. 'It was tough at first. We had to wait for Mitchell and Barry to leave with the others, because I know Mitchell still holds a flame for me. And I had to explain it to Alan.'

'And Shaun?'

'Yeah.'

'And what about Ben?'

'Oh, we never really got off the ground. It was just a drink in the pub.'

Bonnie laughed. 'I don't know how you manage it.'

'Ah, it's the mystery, see. Thing is, now I've de-robed, there's not so much excitement. No one's been paying me any attention these last couple of days.'

'Well, the trenchcoat would raise eyebrows, particularly in a café with pink décor.'

Debbie patted the jacket she wore. It was still black, but a far cry from the ankle-length vampire suit she preferred. Ending at her waist, it allowed people to see her jeans, and unzipped, it gave a view of her staff t-shirt with a smiling anthropomorphic marshmallow on the front.

'I know you think I've changed,' Debbie said. 'You think I'm turning into a pop idol or whatever, but I'll never truly turn to the light. Not on the inside.'

'We have to keep real to what we are.'

'Right.'

They sipped their wine in silence for a while, listening to the patter of snow, the distant laughter, the swaying of the trees.

'What are you going to get me?' Debbie asked at last. 'For Christmas, I mean.'

Bonnie laughed. 'Well, I was in the music shop in Quim a few days ago, and I saw some nice folk CDs….'

'Seriously, don't go there.'

'I stopped short of actually purchasing anything.'

'Just a tube of black nail polish and a four-pack of stout will do.'

'I'll make a note.'

'And what do you want?'

Bonnie sighed. 'Nothing. I have everything I could have dreamed of right here.'

Debbie narrowed her eyes. 'Are you sure?'

'I think so. Things are going pretty well. I have friends, both new and old, I'm the master of my own destiny—'

'Don't lie to me.'

'I'm not!'

'Yes, you are.' Debbie held up a hand and grabbed her forefinger. 'Firstly, your kids. Have you had so much as a phone call since we came here?'

'To be fair, they probably don't know the number—'

'No excuse. And now you've cleared all the negativity out of your head, you're in a position to start thinking about—'

Bonnie put up a hand. 'Oh, no. Don't even mention it.'

'Come on, Bon,' Debbie said, finishing her wine and pouring another glass. 'You're not exactly a dinosaur. And that uniform takes years off you.'

'One or two maybe.'

'More like ten or twenty. I wouldn't go as far as to call you a fox, but you're definitely in the vixen category.'

'Um, thanks. I think.'

'Did you pop into the Thistle when you were in Quim?'

Bonnie shook her head, feeling a sudden flush in her cheeks. It was probably just the wine. Yes, definitely the wine. 'I didn't have time.'

'Yeah, right. Social contact avoidance. I saw Thomas the other day. We had a chat.'

Bonnie's ears burned. 'About what.'

'Oh, the weather. What vegetables were on sale in the grocer's. The usual things.'

'That's nice.'

'He mentioned his dad.'

'Really?'

'He told me that he worries when he goes off to university. He worries about his dad. He said that even though it's been a couple of years since his mum died, his dad still struggles.'

'What's that got to do with me? I mean, I feel sorry for his loss and everything—'

'I suggested that he encourage his dad to ask you out on a date.'

Bonnie sat up, nearly knocking over her glass. 'You did not—'

'I absolutely did. We both agreed that the pair of you need a push in the right direction.'

Bonnie stood up. 'I will not be match-made for your amusement.'

'Sit down, Bon. We still have half a bottle to get through.'

With a sigh, Bonnie slumped back into her seat. 'I

mean, I like him and everything, but he's got a lot of history.'

'He's got baggage. So? You have, too. But, you're both independent, both business owners now. No one's going to be scrimping off the other. You can have a nice, mature, independent relationship.'

'What if he doesn't like me?'

'So you are interested. I thought so.'

Bonnie rolled her eyes. 'Damn, it's the wine talking.'

'You've only drunk half a glass.'

'I don't have your capacity.'

'Look, make whatever excuses you like, but I don't think it would do you any harm at all to go on a date. I know you're enjoying running the café and everything, but it's just work. And you've busted your guts getting it off the ground. You need to let your hair down sometimes. You might even enjoy yourself.'

'I'll think about it.' Bonnie shrugged. 'Not like there'd be much point if the park closes in January.'

'That's not going to happen. Trust me.'

'It's out of your control. And mine. And anyone's, by the look of things.'

'Do you really think your grandfather could be alive somewhere?'

Bonnie had told Debbie what Belinda had said. While Debbie had been skeptical, they had both agreed such a situation was technically possible. Perhaps, like some long-distance overlord, Bonnie's geriatric grandfather was watching over them. From where, however, was the problem. Despite her best efforts to locate him, she had so far drawn a blank.

The wine had started to go to Bonnie's head. 'I think I'll call it a night.'

Debbie smiled. 'Let's finish this up. Isn't this great,

though?' She flapped a hand at the slowly falling snow as it began to fill in footprints and top up heaps alongside the paths. The park lights shone through it, turning it into a glittering spectacle of colour set against the dark of the forest pushing in from the park's boundaries.

'These are the best moments,' Bonnie said. 'Sitting here in the quiet, listening to the wind, thinking back at all the people who came in and left with a smile ... I mean, it's exhausting, but it sure beats swiping tins of beans any day of the week.'

'Or standing in a dole queue,' Debbie said, voice starting to slur, likely a concoction of the wine and the same tiredness that was making Bonnie long for her bed. 'Your grandfather wouldn't shut us down, would he? We've only just got here.'

'No idea. Not like I can ask him.'

Debbie grinned drunkenly. 'Why don't you write a letter to Father Christmas? Tell him you've been a good girl and your wish this year is for the park to stay open.'

'Don't be ridiculous. I wouldn't even know where to address it to.'

'The same place all the kids do. Father Christmas, North Pole. Let the post office figure out the rest.'

'It's a stupid idea.'

'So is a year-round Christmas theme park. But it works.'

They finished off the wine, their conversation turning to more casual things. It was nearly midnight when they headed inside, both shivering with cold on the outside, but lit from within by the wine and a bag of leftover marshmallows Debbie had brought out. They wished each other good night at the top of the stairs. Debbie went into her room, but Bonnie went into the kitchen, aware that if she went to bed without a glass of water, she'd feel terrible in the morning.

A glass of water turned into a coffee. Still feeling tipsy, Bonnie found herself sitting at the table in the living room, scribbling down a note on a piece of writing paper left lying around. Her head was spinning so much that she wasn't entirely sure what she was writing, but she signed off with *P.S. A boyfriend would also be nice, but don't worry if you're busy.* Then closing and sealing the letter, she addressed it as Debbie had suggested, and left it on the side to be posted in the morning.

It was silly, of course it was. But, it was nearly Christmas. A person could dream, couldn't they?

34

STUCK IN THE SNOW

BONNIE FELT TERRIBLE IN THE MORNING. SHE WAS AWARE from the sunlight streaming in through her window that she had dramatically overslept. Rolling out of bed, she nearly tripped and hit her head on the bedside table, just managing to miss it as her feet fell out from under her.

From outside the door came the unforgiving roar of the hoover. She staggered down the hall to the kitchen and found Debbie, already in uniform, in the middle of cleaning up. A bin liner stood next to the kitchen bar, and a wet cloth lay squeezed on the counter top. The air smelled faintly of disinfectant.

'Don't worry,' Debbie said, giving Bonnie a wide smile that defied the laws of alcohol consumption Bonnie was starting to realise she needed to consider a little more, 'Larry's opening up. You take a rest until after lunch, if you like.'

'What's going on?'

'It's bins day, in case you forgot. I figured you weren't likely to be up to it, so I took charge. Plus, I figured I might as well give the place a once over.'

Bonnie had a sudden moment of realisation. She looked at the coffee table where she had left the letter, but it was gone, the surface shining from a fresh polish. She glanced back at the bin bag, stuffed full of old papers and kitchen waste, and gave a shrug.

It had only been a pipedream anyway.

~

The next couple of weeks flew past. The park, fully booked for overnight stays and flooded with day visitors, was a roaring success. Bonnie found herself worked off her feet, crawling into bed each night with the buzz of conversation still in her ears, and the thrill of having made dozens of people happy. It was exhausting work, though, particularly now that they were expanding into doing birthday parties and other private bookings in the small function room around the back. Debbie had proved adept at such work, but even with Christmas just a few days away, Bonnie knew that both of them had to take a step back or face burning out. One evening, a week or so before Christmas, Bonnie decided they should have a meeting.

'We've got to cash in, Bon,' Debbie said, after they reviewed the takings figures. 'After Christmas things will inevitably slow down. Got to get them in the door while we can.'

'All this managing people stuff is pretty new for me,' Bonnie said. 'I'm not sure quite whether I'm doing it right. I mean, are you happy with your pay and conditions?'

Debbie laughed. 'Yeah, it's all good. However, I do need to tell you something.'

'Sure. What is it?'

'After we're done with Christmas, I want to head back to the smoke for a bit.'

'You mean, go home?'

'Just for a few months. I like it here, but … the music scene isn't all that. I'm missing the gigs, and in summer you get the festival circuit. I'll totally be back again in the autumn, perhaps around Halloween.'

Bonnie felt like someone had kicked her in the gut. 'You're leaving?'

'I want to be seasonal, that's all. There's not enough going on in this forest to keep me interested all year round.'

Bonnie decided there was no point bringing up the point that the park would probably be shutting in January anyway. They had both been over it to death. Still, the thought of losing her best friend—

'So, what I was thinking was, I want to have a going away party.'

'Really?'

'Yeah, a big knees up in the café. Next Saturday night.'

'But I thought you wanted to stay until January?'

Debbie looked awkward. 'Yeah, I do, but I want to get it out of the way, you know? Before the Christmas rush kicks in.'

'Okay … that's weird, but whatever you want.'

'And I want it to be fancy dress.'

'What?'

'Totally crazy stuff, anything goes. Everyone's invited.'

'Right.'

'And so I've ordered something special.'

'Okay….'

'And I need you to go and pick it up on Saturday morning.'

'Me? Why me?'

'Because it's my party, and I want it the way I want it. If I go off to collect my costume, you might put up the wrong colour streamers, or buy in the wrong brand of stout from the pub. I need to oversee it all, to make sure it's done right. Don't worry, I'll be fine.'

'I'm not worried about you. Where do I have to get your costume from?'

'Kendal.'

'Seriously?'

'Yeah, well, you have a car and all that so it shouldn't be a problem.'

'No, but—'

'Thanks, Bon. You're the best. I'll give you an address and everything.'

'What kind of costume is it?'

'Oh, you'll see. It's the best. Trust me.'

'I'm starting to run out of trust cards, but I suppose I could lay out one more.' Bonnie shook her head. 'Saturday. Kendal. Right, well, I had nothing else to do on my day off.'

'Cheers, Bon. You're my best friend forever.'

～

The thought of Debbie leaving had rather dampened things for Bonnie, but over the next few days she adjusted to the idea. While Bonnie had slipped into the lifestyle of a café owner at Christmas Land with consummate ease, Debbie, even squeezed into the café uniform, was a fish out of water, missing her home comforts. It would be a shame to see her friend go, but she had got friendly with other members of the community, as well as a couple of people she had bumped into on her regular trips into Quimbeck. In less than two months, she felt more at home here than she ever had in Weston super Mare.

Business was busy right up to the weekend, so by Saturday the 19th, with just a week to go until Christmas,

Bonnie was happy enough to drive into Kendal to pick up Debbie's costume. Debbie had written down an address, and had even checked the time of Bonnie's train into Quim where she had left her car. As she prepared to set out, Debbie lingered by the door, her phone in hand, looking nervous.

'Don't worry,' Bonnie said, slinging her bag over her shoulder. 'It'll be fine. I'll be back in a couple of hours.'

'This is life and death, Bon,' Debbie said. 'Don't miss that train, otherwise you might hit the morning rush hour, and then what will I wear?'

'Relax.'

Debbie shook her head. 'I can't. Go, go, go.'

Smiling to herself over her friend's excessive urgency, Bonnie headed out, walking to Ings Forest station through a light snow and catching the train to Quim. There, she found her car in the Christmas Land car park and headed for Kendal. There was only one real road in and out of Quim, and Debbie had been insistent that Bonnie take it. She thought about trying to find a scenic route through the farming lanes, but she didn't really know the area, and she wanted to get back as quickly as possible. Plus, it was beginning to snow more heavily, and the last thing she wanted was to end up getting stuck in a snowdrift somewhere. It was her day off, after all.

She had just crested the rise of the fell looming above the town, when a figure stepped out of a farm gateway and waved at her. As she slowed down, she saw to her surprise that it was Len.

She stopped and wound down the passenger side window. Len, frowning, leaned inside.

'Hello, Bonnie,' he said. 'Where are you off to?'

'Well, I was just heading into Kendal. I have to pick something up for Debbie.'

'Oh, really?'

'What are you doing here?'

Len shook his head. 'Thomas wanted to go out on a hike this morning, despite the obvious snow. Perhaps for a city boy like him, he thought it would be pretty. He left me a message to meet him right here at ten o'clock, but it's nearly half past and he hasn't shown up. I tried calling him but I couldn't get through. He said he was planning to go to Landerwater, over the fell there, but I'm wondering whether I missed him and he's gone on already.'

Bonnie found her mouth working without conscious thought. 'It's on the way,' she said. 'I can drop you there if you like.'

Len's face brightened. 'Could you really? I wouldn't want to trouble you. Not with it snowing like it is.'

Bonnie took a quick glance around the inside of the car, checking for imperfections. It needed a hoovering, but was otherwise clean enough.

'Sure,' she said. 'Get in.'

Len shook the snow off his jacket and climbed into her tiny Metro. He seemed to double in size as he squeezed in beside her, thanking her as he settled into the seat.

As she slipped the car into gear her sleeve brushed the arm of his coat. Rather than flinch away, Len just gave an awkward grin.

'I really appreciate this,' he said. 'It almost feels like fate that you came along when you did.'

Bonnie's cheeks burned. She scrambled to switch on the air-conditioning, despite the snow falling outside. 'Um, why's that?'

'Well, I managed to walk up here, but I caught my ankle on a root just a little way back down the road. I was prepared to limp over to Landerwater if necessary, but I wasn't looking forward to it.'

'Surely a bus would have come along soon anyway?'

'They don't run in the snow. No one goes out in conditions like this, because you never know how bad it can get.' He gave her a sympathetic smile. 'All the locals know that.'

Bonnie winced. 'Well, I suppose I'm not really local yet.'

'It's okay. I'm glad you're not.'

'Why?' Bonnie blurted, immediately feeling stupid. 'I mean, um, why not?'

'Um, well, because … oh, dear. Look at that.'

Up ahead, shapes were appearing out of the snow, moving towards them. They looked like huge lopping ghosts, and Bonnie felt a moment of panic. Then, the first of the cows appeared out of the falling snow, and she let out her breath.

'I don't believe it,' she said. 'Not again.'

'Just wait,' Len said. 'They'll be past us in a minute or two.'

They watched as the cows jostled past the car, some bumping against the sides. It was taking far longer for the herd to pass than it had the last time, on the day Bonnie and Debbie had arrived. Just as Bonnie was thinking there surely couldn't be any more animals to come, the cows stopped moving, coming to rest beside their car, mooing and jostling with each other as they bumped against the windows.

'Um, that's not good,' Len said.

Bonnie peered over her shoulder. She had pulled into a small passing place, but hadn't gone close enough to the hedge to prevent the cows from surrounding them on all sides. She looked at Len.

'Will they kick or get upset if we try to get out?'

Len shrugged. 'I have no idea.'

'But you grew up around here, didn't you?'

'Yes, but I've never been a farmer. They look docile enough, but I wouldn't want to make them annoyed.'

They sat in silence for a few minutes. The cows didn't move, continuing their frustrated mooing while snow pattered down.

Len pulled up a bag he had put on the floor between his legs, a little hiker's rucksack. He looked up at Bonnie and smiled as he withdrew a small flask.

'Can I interest you in a brew?' he said. 'I've got a spare cup.'

'I can't, I'm driving. Well, hopefully at some point.'

Len smiled. 'It's tea.'

'Oh, well in that case, sure.'

Len unscrewed the lid and pulled a second cup out of his bag. Balancing one on the dashboard, he poured Bonnie a steaming cup of tea and passed it across. She held it with both hands, appreciating the warmth.

'Not what I had planned for my Saturday,' Len said. 'Although being stuck in a car with you is probably better than trudging through the snow. Just don't wind down the windows.'

'Thanks. I think.'

'It was meant as a compliment.'

Bonnie held up the cup. 'And you make a fine cup of tea. Not too plasticky.'

'I'm glad.'

Ignoring the cows standing at the windows, they began to talk of random things, the words coming easily as they relaxed into each others' presence. Before she knew it, Bonnie had progressed from talking about the café menu and how she had decided on the colours for the new uniforms to her fears over whether her children would accept her new life, and why her marriage had failed. Len listened with barely an interruption unless she asked him for his opinion, his eyes holding hers, his interest sharp. In the end the conversation came around to the passing of his wife, and the hurt it had caused.

'I wasn't sure I could ever move on,' he said. 'For months I was in a total shutdown state, unable to see anything in front of me. It was the pub that brought me through it, the sense of community, and Thomas, who was a rock. I couldn't have done it without him.'

'And how do you feel now?'

Len sighed, but his eyes twinkled with light. 'At first I always focused on my loss. Over time I came to turn it around, to focus on what we had for so many years. To remember the good days and forget the bad. To celebrate, rather than grieve. And in time I came to realise that while she was gone, I was still here. While I can't ever bring her back, she wouldn't want me to spend the rest of my life grieving for her. She would want me to be happy, to move on. It was just that I hadn't met anyone else.'

Bonnie noticed the use of the past tense. 'And you, um, have now?'

Len's cheeks glowed. He wiped sweat off his forehead and stared at his cup. The flask was empty; they had drunk three small cups each. Somehow, more than an hour had passed while they waited surrounded by cows.

'Maybe I, um, wondered if—'

The car bumped. Bonnie twisted in her seat as a heavy body ground past her window.

'They're moving,' Len said. 'At last.'

The cows began shift, bumping against each other, tails swishing at the falling snow. The road cleared ahead of them, the surface left a churned mess of sludge. Bonnie was staring at it when a hand thumped on her window.

'Lass!'

She wound down the window. Reg Coldsworth, his flat cap flecked with snow, gave her a toothy grin.

'Me apologies for leaving you stuck like that. Taking the lasses here in to the shed but a tree went down. Boys just got it cut. Have to tell yee the snow's pretty heaped up ahead. You ain't going nowhere on those tyres. Stay put and I'll send a lad up with the tractor to give yee a tow. Oh, get on, Len. Didn't see you in there. Bit of a date, is it?' Cackling, Reg tapped the door of the car then headed on after his departing cows. Bonnie, cheeks burning even worse than before, wound the window back up.

'So, do we believe him, or do we chance it?' she said.

'It's your car.'

Bonnie put the car into gear, feeling a strange reluctance as she did so that she was breaking a moment she might never get back. The car started forward, but as soon as it hit the churned mess on the road, the wheels began to spin. Feeling an uncanny sense of relief, she put the car into neutral and put the handbrake back on.

'I guess we're stuck here,' she said.

Len grinned. 'Looks like it.' He reached into his bag. 'Would you like a piece of cake? I was saving it in case we were stuck overnight, but I suppose we might as well eat it while we can still enjoy the taste.'

'Overnight? I hope not.'

Len laughed. 'We're only about a mile out of Quim. We could hike it if you like.'

She held his gaze for a couple of seconds longer than felt normal, then shook her head. 'No, I think we'd better stay here and wait for the tractor. We wouldn't want him to waste a journey.'

'Cake it is, then.'

35

HAPPY ENDINGS

THE TRACTOR TOOK ITS SWEET TIME TO ARRIVE. BY THE time it came chugging up the road, the day was slipping away, and any chance of going to Kendal to pick up Debbie's costume was gone.

Not that Bonnie had thought much about it. The hours had passed in light conversation with Len, the pair becoming increasingly at ease with each other, even though by the time the tractor did show up, she was bursting for the toilet but afraid to say so. From the increasingly tense look on Len's face, she suspected that he was, too.

The tractor towed them back down the road to Quimbeck, leaving them in the pub car park. After they had both made a quite obvious run for their respective toilets, they met again in the warm confines of the bar, where a smiling Thomas was polishing glasses ready for opening time. After apologising to his father for leaving him stranded in a way which seemed a little suspicious, he poured them both a drink and then made an excuse to attend to some jobs in the private bar around the back.

'Well, that was an adventure,' Len said. 'You know, it's

getting late, so if you'd rather stay in Quim, I think one of the guest rooms is free.'

'That's kind of you, but I really should get back,' Bonnie said, nevertheless feeling the urge to stay in Len's warm company. 'But, you know, today was fun. We should, ah....'

'Try it again sometime? Only not in the middle of nowhere?'

'Sounds great, I'd love to.'

'You know, there are some nice restaurants in Quim—'

'Sounds great,' Bonnie blurted, momentarily losing her composure. They both laughed. The ease with which it came was comforting.

'I'd better be getting back,' Bonnie said. 'Just in case Debbie turned my café into a rock club or something.'

'It's dark,' Len said, even though with the proliferation of street lights in Quim, it never really was. 'I'll walk you to the station.'

And he did. Before boarding the train, they didn't share anything as clichéd as a first kiss, but Len did give her hand a quick squeeze and told her he hoped to see her again soon.

She was almost at Ings Forest station before her heartbeat had slowed down, and by the time she reached the park gates, she was humming to herself, skipping along like Julie Andrews in *The Sound of Music*.

It was a surprise that neither Brendon nor the elves were on duty by the gates. It was past the park's official closing time but even so, someone was usually around at this time of night. June's shop and café, too, was closed early.

Bonnie wondered if something was up. Perhaps there had been a power outage. She headed for the café to find out if a similar problem had affected her own business.

She was nearing the plaza when she saw Debbie walking towards her.

'Bon! There you are! Fancy seeing you out here at this time of night.'

Bonnie frowned, then remembered why she had gone out in the car in the first place. 'I'm sorry, I couldn't get your costume. I had a little trouble with the car.'

Debbie patted her on the shoulder. 'Quite all right. No problem. In fact, I'm good with what I'm wearing right now. How about you? Do you need to change?'

Bonnie frowned. 'What's going on? Why are you acting all strange?'

Debbie gave a nervous laugh. 'Well, um, you see, while you were out, I did some thinking. Are you okay with a private chat?'

'About what?'

'Oh, this and that. In the café?'

'Right now?'

'Um, yes. Right now.' Debbie put an arm around Bonnie and steered her towards the plaza. The café's lights were off, the windows dark.

'Is there some problem with the power?'

'No, not that I know of.'

'Perhaps we should go over to the pub?'

'No, no. No. Absolutely not. The café is fine.' Debbie was practically hauling Bonnie forward, fingers squeezing tight around her arm.

'Look, what's this all about?'

'I'll tell you when we get inside.'

Debbie pulled the door open and pushed Bonnie forward into the gloom. Immediately she knew something was different; the air felt wrong: too warm, oppressive, sweaty—

'SURPRISE!' came the roar of several dozen voices as

in a single moment the lights came on, party poppers exploded and hands began to clap. They were all there, Brendon and June, Niall, Jason, Belinda, Larry, the elves, Ben and even Gene in Father Christmas costume, albeit sitting on a chair in the corner. A few regular customers too, everyone she had got to know over the last few weeks, all cheering for her.

Hanging over the counter, a colourful sign: THANK YOU, BONNIE.

And a girl pushing through the crowd, slender and attractive, braids in her hair and glitter on her cheeks, reaching out to embrace her.

'Claire….'

'Hi Mum. Glad I could make it. Can't believe what you've done here. Awesome.'

And then, as she pulled away, a little boy came running forward, seven years old, arms outstretched.

'Timothy….'

'Hi Grandma. Merry Christmas.'

She hugged her grandson to her, and looked up into the face of the man coming behind him. His smile told her everything she needed to know, and in that moment she was prepared to channel all the spirit she needed to forgive and forget, and to move forward with their lives.

'Mum, I'm sorry I was an ass,' Steve said. 'Debbie called me and gave me a sound ear bashing. I was a real idiot.'

'Give me a hug,' Bonnie said, pulling him close, then reached out and pulled Claire in beside him while Timothy still clung to her waist.

'Merry Christmas,' Bonnie said, tears in her eyes. Glancing up, her vision clearing for just a moment, she caught sight of Debbie standing by the counter, a smile on her face, and she began to cry all over again.

'Coffee's up,' Debbie said as Bonnie appeared out of her bedroom. 'You're still alive?'

Bonnie grinned. 'Best party ever. And all thanks to you.'

'Ah, it would have sucked if no one had shown up. I went round the park while you were out, slipping everyone a fiver.'

'How on earth did you get hold of my kids? I couldn't even contact them.'

Debbie grinned. 'I know the internet a bit better than you. There's no such thing as off-the-grid these days.'

'I suppose not. I still can't believe it.'

'I just wanted you to know how much you're appreciated,' Debbie said. 'And I know a lot of the guys around here did too, they just didn't know how to show it.' With a grin, she added, 'Luckily I'm here.'

'You did a great job.'

Debbie shifted from foot to foot. 'So … any news?'

'What news?'

'With Len?'

Bonnie rolled her eyes. 'We might go out for dinner.'

Debbie clicked her fingers. 'Nice one. Thomas said you looked pretty pleased with yourselves—'

'Hang on a minute. Thomas?' Bonnie narrowed her eyes. 'Was yesterday a set up?'

'No … well, I mean, Reg Coldsworth's hot chocolates are on the house for the next six months. Nice old guy, don't you think?'

'I can't believe you.'

'Oh, and you got post. It arrived this morning.' Debbie held up a letter.

'What's this?'

'Read it.'

Bonnie took the letter and turned it over. The brown envelope had a paper chain design around the outside and a little postmark of a smiling snowman in the corner.

'It's from the North Pole. But I never—'

'I posted it,' Debbie said. 'You think I'd throw away a letter to Father Christmas? What kind of bad karma do you think I'm looking for?'

'But—'

'Just read it.'

Bonnie turned it over. The seal seemed soft, loose.

'I um, steamed it open,' Debbie said. 'But I promise, it's like the last time ever. I'll never do it again. Just read it. Come on, hurry up.'

Bonnie pulled out the letter and unfolded it. On a single sheet of ornate paper, neat handwriting read:

Dear Bonnie,

How lovely to hear from you. I'm surprised you knew where to find me, after all I've led a quiet life all these years. Thank you for taking on the responsibilities of Mervin's café and bringing life back to Christmas Land.

I'm afraid it had begun to stagnate, but in your hands, I think it will prosper for years to come. If my legs were a little more mobile, I'd be tempted to visit, but I'm happy enough here in Lapland, doing what I do for whatever time I have left. Perhaps in the new year, when things have settled down, you could come and visit me! In the meantime, you take care of yourself, and take care of my park. When I'm gone, it will become your park, and I hope you will let it continue bringing happiness to so many people. I leave it in your wise and careful hands.

Goodbye now, and Merry Christmas!

Yours sincerely,

Grandfather

P.S. I can't promise about the boyfriend, but I'll see what I can do.

Bonnie looked up. 'I found him,' she whispered. 'And he answered.'

'And he's keeping the park open,' Debbie said, barely able to keep her feet on the ground as she bounced up and down, one hand on the kitchen counter. 'You did it, Bon.'

'Not alone, I didn't,' Bonnie said, looking up. 'You were with me every step of the way.'

Debbie shrugged. 'Well, someone had to look after you, didn't they?' Lifting a hand and counting on her fingers she said, 'Today's agenda. You relax and watch a Christmas movie while I clean up the café downstairs. You go off with your kids and enjoy the day while I flirt with Larry and sell marshmallows and hot chocolate. And then me and you head into Quim in the evening to check out the best restaurants for Len to take you on your first proper date next week.'

'Isn't he supposed to choose the restaurant?'

Debbie rolled her eyes. 'What is this, the nineteen fifties? You've got to get with the times, my dear.'

Bonnie smiled and raised her coffee. 'I'll drink to that.'

'To us and the café, and the future,' Debbie said.

Bonnie laughed. 'And Merry Christmas.'

END

Merry Christmas

ACKNOWLEDGMENTS

Big thanks as always to those of you who provided help and encouragement. A special thanks to Elizabeth Mackey for the cover, my magnificent editorial team Jenny and Nick, and to Jenny Twist, my muse, for your eternal support.

In addition, extra thanks goes to my Patreon supporters, in particular to Rosemary Kenny, Jane Ornelas, Sean Flanagan, Alan MacDonald, Anja Peerdeman, Sharon Kenneson, Jenny Brown, Leigh McEwan, Amaranth Dawe, and Janet Hodgson.

You guys are awesome.

Milton Keynes UK
Ingram Content Group UK Ltd.
UKHW040703201123
432908UK00001B/68